BATTLETECH:
FOX TALES
THE COLLECTED FOX PATROL STORIES

BY BRYAN YOUNG

BATTLETECH: FOX TALES
Edited by John Helfers
Cover art by Ken Coleman
Interior art by Alan Blackwell, Brent Evans, Harri Kallio, Chris Lewis, Duane Loose,
    Matt Plog, Franz Vohwinkel
Cover design by David Kerber

Printed in USA.

Published by Catalyst Game Labs,
an imprint of InMediaRes Productions, LLC
5003 Main St. #110 • Tacoma, WA 98407

FOREWORD

As the editor of *Shrapnel*, the Official *BattleTech* Magazine, I love reading through submissions and finding a little unexpected gem of a story. It's honestly my favorite part of the job. There is a certain tone, feel, and expectation to most *BattleTech* stories—par for the course for stories about military sci-fi tales about giant, stompy war robots—but every once in a while, I come across a tale that blows me away for one reason or another, often by subverting one or more of these expectations without denying the essence of what truly makes it fit in the *BattleTech* universe. Maybe the style or character voice is different. Maybe the writing is breathtaking. And sometimes what grabs me is the central character, someone unlike any *BattleTech* protagonist we've ever seen.

That last instance was the case with "The Secret Fox," the very first story in this collection. Katie Ferraro isn't your usual *BattleTech* protagonist by any means. She isn't a hard-bitten middle-aged mercenary, jaded by decades of warfare. She isn't an opportunist just looking for a payday. She is young and idealistic, and instead of looking at the bottom line, she takes contracts because she genuinely wants to help people. Katie is the kind of character who remains true to herself and to everyone she loves, because she cannot be anything different.

When "The Secret Fox" crossed my desk in 2020, I was already familiar with Bryan due to working on his novel *Honor's Gauntlet* earlier that year, so I suspected I would like this story. But I had no idea what I was in for, and I loved every moment of it. Now, two years later, the trials and travails of the Fox Patrol have become a regular staple of *Shrapnel*, and readers eagerly await the next installment. My first indication of how well this series had resonated was seeing a photo of a *Kit Fox* miniature painted in Fox Patrol colors, and it brought a tear to my eye to see this series leap off the page and into real life.

I am humbled to have had even a small part in helping bring this series out, and I hope you enjoy the story gems in this collection as much as I did.

—PHILIP A. LEE

INTRODUCTION

As much as being a MechWarrior was a dream of Katie's, getting to create a mercenary unit like The Fox Patrol in the *BattleTech* universe was a dream of mine. Thankfully, my editors—John Helfers and Philip A. Lee—were delighted to indulge me as I kept turning these novellas in for publication in *Shrapnel.*

As the story grew, so too did my love for Katie and her ragtag team. They're a diverse group of folks who have no business being mercenaries in a world as rough-and-tumble as *BattleTech*, but that's why I love them. Katie has a heart and cares deeply about all of the MechWarriors in her command. They're a found family, and those seem to be the most important families in my experience.

This whole enterprise grew from a single idea I had, an image in my head I couldn't shake. I had this singular image of a young woman swimming in a lake and diving into the middle and finding a 'Mech just beneath the surface. There was something striking about the glint of sun off the water and the freedom of swimming. When I played the *MechWarrior* games on the SNES, my favorite tactic was to help manage my heat by parking my ass in the nearest lake and firing with abandon from there, so thinking a 'Mech pilot could die there, hiding in the water waiting to ambush some unsuspecting foe, felt very plausible to me. All of it was in service of getting this young woman, dreaming of being a MechWarrior, a 'Mech of her own in a way that made sense.

When I pitched this story to the editors, they immediately nixed the lake and told me to go back to the drawing board. I worked my hardest to find another angle and that's the story that opens this collection. It has threads of excitement that I love in it, and is matched with Hogarth's enthusiasm for finding his own *Iron Giant.*

Funnily enough, I never heard back when I sent the pitch back for approval. I was talking to Michael A. Stackpole (of "Stackpoling" fame in *BattleTech*) and he said, "Just write the story. If it's good, they'll print it. Better to ask forgiveness than permission."

For reasons beyond me, I listened to him. And instead of waiting, I fired off that first story to Phil and he loved it enough to include it in the third installment of *Shrapnel.* The rest was history. I loved writing Katie so much, I immediately began work on the next story. And the next. And the next. I loved adding Arkee and Evan to the mix, two of my favorite characters to write in *BattleTech.* And then Nicks and Ramirez followed. And then Frankie. I love them all so much, and have such high hopes for their future.

And the fact that folks seem to like these stories is an utter delight. Even among the editors. The fourth story in this collection, "A Fox on Galatea," even went into a custody dispute between John and Phil. John had asked me for a novella set on Galatea, and I sent him this Fox Patrol story, and he and Phil fought over who got to print it because Phil felt it belonged in *Shrapnel.* Phil ultimately won, but it was nice to know the powers at be at Catalyst were excited about these stories, too.

I'm so proud to have this collection of stories in one place, and to have been able to add this fifth story. "The Fox Hunt" offers a new window into what the future holds for the Fox Patrol, and I can't wait for you all to see what that is. It's going to be a lot of fun. I promise.

—Bryan Young

*This is for the folks on the margins dreaming of a better life.
Like Katie, I hope they find their 'Mech in the jungle.*

"The cunning of the fox is as murderous as the violence of the wolf."

—Thomas Paine

ONE
THE SECRET FOX

"I had the dream again," Katie Ferraro said, but she was sure Scarecrow wasn't listening.

Scarecrow wasn't his real name, but that's what everyone in old Potsdam called him. He wasn't terribly scary, but he did have the sharp beak and black, bushy eyebrows like you might expect a crow to have.

His hand was out, taking the wrench she held up for him. "The MechWarrior dream again?"

"Yes." She smiled, and her eyes focused in on the lumbering AgroMech they worked on, wishing it were a BattleMech. "I was piloting a *Catapult*, skipping along toward a battle. I felt like I *was* the 'Mech. Every move I made, the 'Mech responded. My legs were the 'Mech's legs. My arms..." She paused, thinking for a second. *Catapult*s didn't have arms, per se. "Well, my arms were just part of the 'Mech. I didn't need them. Why would I?"

"*Catapult*. That's an old 'Mech. Long time since anyone's seen one of those 'round these parts," Scarecrow said, his head disappearing behind the maintenance compartment as he went back to tinker.

"It's been a long time since anyone's seen *any* real 'Mechs around here, Scarecrow."

"True enough, that is," he said. "At least since the bombs fell. Don't expect to see any more, either. Least not ones that aren't already here. The old battered up 'Mechs that got left behind."

Those battered up 'Mechs, BattleMechs and WorkMechs alike, were the bread and butter of Scarecrow's service. Since they were all held together with spit and baling wire, Scarecrow's shop never wanted for business. And since he made the proverbial house calls, there was almost always something to work on.

Katie frowned. "I just want to be a MechWarrior."

"No, you don't. It's hot, messy work. Lethal, too. MechWarriors from backwaters never last long. You don't want to waste your life gettin' shot up as a mercenary for who-knows-what for not enough pay. You're young. Got your whole life ahead of you."

"I'm seventeen," she said, a sing-song trace of defiance in her voice.

"And how many seventeen-year-olds you know got themselves apprenticed to a 'Mech tech?"

She toed the metal scaffolding grate in front of her. Sheepish. Katie knew she should be grateful. Scarecrow wasn't just her boss; he'd taken her in the year before. After her parents had died in the accident. They'd fostered her dream of being a MechWarrior, and they were the ones who had arranged the apprenticeship. They knew how important her dreams were, and on Jerangle, they knew Scarecrow was the closest she could come to touching them. This was probably the closest she'd ever get to working with 'Mechs in the backwater of a planet that had been written off by the Inner Sphere. They both knew it.

She put her hand on the AgroMech's construction-yellow arm as though she were consoling a living, breathing person. If she'd been born in another time, then maybe she would have had a chance to live those dreams.

But not right now.

Not in the 3140s.

All the excitement and conflict of the Inner Sphere passed Jerangle by. At least since the borders were more settled, and everyone seemed to have their eyes on something bigger than the smallest holdings in the Lyran Commonwealth. And there didn't look to be any chance of that changing. Not any time soon.

The most she'd ever see of new BattleMechs would be the occasional mercenary unit that blew into town for the odd job here or there. But even those were few and far between. Rarer still were visits from the Lyran military. It was like they didn't even remember Jerangle existed.

No. Jerangle was quiet.

"Hand me that spanner," Scarecrow told her.

She knew which one he meant. Maybe she'd even guessed he'd need it soon, since she'd already pulled it from the toolbox and held it, waiting for his request. Handing it to him, she stepped around to watch him ratchet the bolts back on the assembly for the AgroMech's shoulder joint.

He must have sensed the unease in her voice. "We've got to get this 'Mech back together and out in the field before lunch. Maybe one day you'll get your dream. But it's not going to be today."

Katie hoped he was wrong.

Katie convinced Scarecrow to let her pilot the AgroMech back to its owners and then give her the rest of the day off. There weren't any 'Mechs left in the bay for repairs, and the next scheduled maintenance on anything wouldn't be until next week.

He'd been reluctant at first, just like when she'd asked to pilot the AgroMech, but he had a hard time saying no when it mattered.

"Just be careful. And don't do anything foolish while you're out there," he told her over the radio as she settled into the AgroMech's command couch. "Can't afford to have anybody thinking ol' Scarecrow's lettin' you out to take risks or nothing. They'll say I've lost my marbles."

"Maybe you have, Scarecrow," she said. She couldn't contain the joy in her voice as she strapped the helmet on and willed the 'Mech forward.

It was a short walk to the outskirts of town where the fields were. They cultivated all sorts of things on Jerangle where the soil was good. Near Potsdam, it was mainly rice. Further into the forests on the other side of town, where the rocky jungle took over, they grew coffee, vanilla, and cacao. The crops all did well in the heat and humidity.

Katie had learned to love the heat herself. She thought growing up in such a place would help prepare her for being a MechWarrior. All the stories she read talked so much about how hot 'Mechs got.

For the AgroMechs she was allowed to pilot, the warmest they got was the ambient temperature of Potsdam.

She was reluctant to deliver the 'Mech. Something inside Katie wished she could just keep driving it. Past the farm, past the outskirts of Potsdam. Past everything. And she'd just find a new life out there, with the AgroMech as her only constant companion. It would be a hard life, but she'd make it work somehow. And once she'd hired her and her trusty 'Mech out for enough work, she'd be able to sell the AgroMech and trade up to a proper BattleMech.

She dreamed of starting her own mercenary company.

One day. She smiled. *One day.*

Instead of fleeing into the sunset, she parked the AgroMech outside of old man Peabody's rice farm and let him know it was back.

"Scarecrow did a great job with it, sir," she told Peabody. "It's running like new again."

Peabody was grateful, of course, and told Katie that he'd settle up with Scarecrow the next day, which was fine by her. It didn't matter to her when Scarecrow got paid as long as he did. She'd get hers soon enough. All she did was save up her money anyway.

That 'Mech wasn't going to buy itself.

With the rest of the day off and only an empty apartment above Scarecrow's shop to go home to, she figured she'd go hiking. It would keep her mind off the yearning in her heart. And she wouldn't die of boredom. She'd read the same books and watched the same shows over and over and over again and they'd lost all their allure.

She began her hike into the jungle from Peabody's farm. She didn't know if it was actually a jungle, but it seemed jungle enough to her. Hot and humid, lots of broad leafy trees and a thick canopy. Vines everywhere. It changed a bit as the land got craggier and led up the mountain, but it was all still very dense. As long as she didn't get into any of the crops beneath the canopy, no one would say boo about her traipsing through the jungle. The kids of Potsdam did it all the time.

Seemed like every year or two, one of them would get lost, and there would be a search party. Katie wouldn't let that happen to her. She had an innate sense of direction. And, occasionally, she cut small marks in trees as she passed, just to be sure she wouldn't get lost.

But getting lost was a thought that haunted her.

She'd already been lost by everything she'd ever loved. She didn't want to get lost from everything else, too.

There were many trails that led to notable places. One led to a waterfall. Another led to a system of caves and an underwater river. Katie tended to avoid that one, though. There had been too many stories of kids swimming into the caves and drowning.

She couldn't drown.

She wanted to die in a BattleMech.

Well, she didn't really want to die at all. But if she had to choose her death, she knew she wanted it to be inside a 'Mech.

That was the only thing that made sense to her.

The hike would be good for her, but she wanted to stay away from the beaten paths. She didn't want to interact with anyone who wasn't a 'Mech or a MechWarrior. And she wouldn't be finding anyone like that on Jerangle, at least not near Potsdam.

Pushing on, she found an opening she could forge on her own. Taking a deep right turn into dense foliage, Katie kicked her way through and walked until she came to the steep gash of a ravine. She knew it to be where the Mindel River cut through the jungle as it headed through Potsdam and out to the sea. She'd never seen the ravine from this high up before. Usually, she'd hike down the other way and see the falls from below.

Perhaps there hadn't been trails up to this spot because people found it dangerous. She let out a series of shallow breaths, doing her best to catch it. After wiping the sweat from her face, Katie pulled her beat-up old canteen from her belt and took a long, cool draught of the water.

Cutting through the jungle without a machete was difficult work. And the bits of her exposed flesh told the tale. She'd been nicked and cut in a dozen places where sharp leaves cut her or branches snagged her. But she had no qualms with the damage. She'd nicked the trees to keep her trail as much as they had nicked her, so it seemed a fair exchange.

She was just grateful to be out. And alive. And alone with her thoughts.

In these quiet times, she daydreamed about BattleMechs as much as she'd dreamed of anything in her nights, and tromping through the jungles reminded her of everything she wanted to do with her life, only from the cockpit of a 'Mech.

Screwing the cap back onto her canteen, she hooked it back onto her belt and took a long look at the ravine before her. The edge stood a few feet from her and she couldn't see the sparkle of the running water below her at that angle, but she could certainly hear its forceful rush. It added a lovely background to the foreground noise of cawing birds.

She stepped forward, inching closer to the edge until she could see the current far below her. A narrow shaft of hot sunlight cut across the chasm and made the water sparkle below it.

Truly a beautiful sight.

She looked up and down the ravine, hoping she could place where along the path she was, but didn't recognize the curve. She might have from an aerial map, just not from her memory. She etched the curve into her mind, hoping to look it up later.

That's when the glint of something silvery caught her eye down below.

Just as the river upstream disappeared, there stood a copse of jungle trees on an embankment on the shore. The trees climbed up to the level where she was, and it would be a hike to get down there. But through those trees, the sun caught metal.

"Metal?" Katie said to herself. There shouldn't be anything metal out here at all.

But as the sun shifted slightly over the course of the minutes she'd been there, she knew her mind wasn't playing tricks on her.

Then her curiosity took the better of her, and she knew she had to investigate.

Looking around, Katie found a tree nearby to nick with her tracking mark and began the hike uphill around the lip of the ravine to make her way down to the trees below and whatever secret they kept.

She divided her attention as she walked between the trees ahead and her feet below. There were definitely parts of her makeshift trail that weren't as solid as others and she'd send rocks tumbling down into the water below. Other times, the path was nonexistent, and she would have to cut into the trees again and walk around and back to the ravine's edge.

Once she finally reached the trees, there was nothing of the metal she could see. The tree canopy blocked any view she would have had of the ground or any metal objects or structures held within.

No. If she wanted to know what was down there, she was going to have to climb down and see for herself.

Lost in the excitement, she didn't even stop to take a breather or drink more water. She simply went to work scanning around for a way down.

With no obvious path, she knew she'd have to climb down. It would be difficult and dangerous. It was ten meters to the floor, easy. And she couldn't tell how soft the ground was, but she'd be working without a net in either case.

Fortunately, her belt was made of tightly wound cord. Scarecrow had given it to her as a gift.

"It's never wise to be caught without essentials anywhere around. Just cut the buckle and *bam!*—fifteen meters of cord for anything you need."

She hadn't thought it a particularly nice gift at the time. She'd needed a belt, true, and she didn't mind the utilitarian nature of it. It was the fact that someone had paid him for a repair with a case of the belts. He'd been wearing one himself when he handed it to her, and she saw them in their packaging, scattered all over the workbench.

She'd laughed about it later, but was grateful for it now.

Unspooling the cord, she didn't quite realize how much was hidden in the weave. Fifteen meters was a lot. But it would be perfect for what she needed to do.

Finding a sturdy tree, she looped the cord around it and tied it into a heavy knot. Then knotted it again for good measure. The last thing she wanted was to rappel down the side and fall to her death because she used the wrong knot.

Satisfied that the rope would hold, she tossed the rest of her former belt down over the edge. There was a narrow gap between the canopy and the rocky wall, so she wouldn't have too much of a problem getting down. She put on the tight leather gloves from her pack and wrapped the cord around her waist, ready to make the descent.

Taking in a deep breath, she hoped no harm would come to her, and that there was something really interesting hidden in the trees to make all the effort worth it.

If there wasn't, she was going to be mighty pissed as she climbed back up the ravine.

The first step over the edge when rappelling was always the most nerve-wracking. It was that first moment of truth that forced you to trust in the work you'd done and the physics of climbing and mountaineering. And the strength in your own arms and legs.

Katie took in a deep breath and descended.

She went slow at first, and felt the broad leaves of the trees scrape against her back as she came down. But she kept her focus on the rope and the rock wall in front of her. She didn't want to put her foot in the wrong hole or smush a snake or kick a bird or anything else. And she certainly didn't want to get her feet stuck. Falling from that height would be bad enough; doing it backward after breaking an ankle wasn't going to be good for anyone.

"You got this, Katie," she told herself.

And she had no reason to believe she was lying.

The ground came up sooner than she expected. She'd been so focused on doing everything correctly, she didn't realize how long she'd been doing it. When she finally took that step onto solid ground and was able to let go of the rope, she stretched her aching fingers, hoping to bring feeling back into them quickly.

Then she bounced on her knees a bit, too, just to get all the blood flowing in all the right places.

She turned around to finally sate her curiosity and wondered if she'd even be able to find anything in the trees. They'd grown into something like a solid wall, a dozen trees, all clumped far too closely together.

"Nuts."

She'd have to trudge further still to satisfy her curiosity.

"This better be worth it."

Katie walked around the immediate wall of trees and found an opening that would let her through. It was a tight squeeze, and she felt like she'd entered a different world.

Dark and swampy. She'd been accustomed to the humidity, but the darkness and proximity to the river and the soft ground had turned the place into as much of a bog as anything. The din of the river was loud, but the noises of the birds had vanished, replaced by the sound of skittering insects and their clicking calls to each other.

Her flesh crawled as much as she imagined the insects were.

Looking up, she tried to see any of the piercing shards of sunlight that had reflected the glint of metal. Pin pricks only, but nothing metal, no shiny reflective surfaces. She would have to delve deeper to find anything.

Winding through another grouping of trees, the light grew even more scarce here. She stepped forward, reaching out in front of her to make sure she didn't bump into anything. She hoped her eyes would adjust to the darkness easier, but she had no such luck.

Reaching out in front of her, she felt something. Smooth. Not like the trees at all, which were rough. And cool to the touch.

It seemed like all the trees and leaves, especially in the more humid pockets like this one, were hot and damp. But this one was cool.

Metal?

Maybe she'd found it.

What she was looking for.

Stepping forward carefully, the tips of her boots found the same thing. She wondered if it was some old, forgotten power relay or transformer box. Maybe it was the remnants of an old hydroelectric plant. Jerangle had been populated for at least six hundred years, and the folks that first settled here could have built anything. It could have been a hundred things, but she wanted to know which one thing it really was.

She felt around, trying to find the edges of it and found that it wasn't large enough to really be a building of any sort. It was too narrow for that, though it was big. And it had a base around it that was wider than that.

Legs?

Katie's heart skipped a beat.

Could it be...?

A 'Mech?

She wasn't that lucky.

But her mind raced with the possibilities. *What if it* is *a 'Mech? How would it have gotten here? Why would it have just been abandoned?*

Trying to find the edges of the 'Mech—she'd already begun to think of it as a 'Mech—she found that it did, indeed have two "legs." Sure, they could have been struts for some ancient treehouse, but how did that even make sense?

Then she wondered about what the spot would have looked like without the grove sprouting up around it. Perhaps, if the river hadn't changed course in a few hundred years and maybe it was some electro plant, this could have been an observation post where someone could have kept an eye on things in both directions of this bend in the river.

But she *wanted* it to be a 'Mech.

That would have been the best of all scenarios. Right?

When she finally made it to the backside and had circumnavigated the entire mysterious object, she realized that she was going to have to climb it.

Cursing under her breath, she wished she hadn't tied her cord so tightly around the tree. Still, she'd be able to get along without it.

Remembering she had a light in her pack, she pulled it out, cursing the whole time. She shone it on the metal structure, and it definitely had hand- and footholds, even though they were grimy with age and covered in moss.

A bolt of excitement jolted her heart.

She smiled as she attached the light to her head with the provided elastic band and began her ascent.

Every meter she climbed, the more the excitement swelled within her.

This couldn't be possible.

But every time her hands found a new hold and her feet pushed her up higher, she knew at least some part of it to be true.

When she reached the cockpit, the light from the trees filtered in better up here, and she felt much more comfortable thinking the word that had her so excited.

BattleMech!

From what she could see, the 'Mech had only limited arms. It was a squat design. She'd have to do more research to find out exactly what kind of 'Mech she was dealing with. But the torso was wider than the legs, and the arms were more weapon than arms. It definitely didn't have hands.

She climbed around to the hatch that would grant her entrance and hoped that she'd be able to get inside. "Open, please."

Her arms were tired from all of her exertions, and she wasn't sure she'd be able to just hang on, clinging to the side of the 'Mech without losing her grip and falling down.

A keypad on the side of the hatch would grant her access, and her heart fell. How could she possibly guess the code of the MechWarrior who had last piloted this gorgeous, if abandoned, machine?

First, she touched the keypad to see if it even still had power. The fusion engines that powered a 'Mech were supposed to provide limitless energy, but there had to be a reason this particular 'Mech had been abandoned in the jungle and overgrown with moss.

Katie smiled when it lit up at her touch.

Her fingers hovered over the keys, wondering what she'd input. But then she remembered a lot of these 'Mechs had maintenance access codes. And she'd studied plenty of those. On the off-chance she'd ever get a hands on an actual 'Mech.

They were long sequences, but she had forced herself to commit them to memory as part of learning 'Mech lore.

The first she tried merely caused the console to beep at her disapprovingly.

The second time yielded the same result.

"Damn it."

But the third time?

Well, the third time worked, and the hatch opened.

The smell was the first, worst thing she noticed. The worst thing her nostrils had ever inhaled. Foul was an understatement. Something must have died and rotted inside the humid heat of the 'Mech's cockpit.

And that made her just the tiniest bit afraid of going in.

The cockpit was dark. The only light came from her headlamp and the faint glow of the buttons and dials on the other side of the command couch.

With her arm and legs weakening, Katie didn't have much of a choice but to head in.

Somehow, being *inside* the cockpit made the stench even worse. She pulled a bandana from her pocket and wrapped it around her nose and mouth. It didn't do much, but it would help some.

She smirked, thinking she'd look like some sort of bandit raiding a 'Mech.

The ache of her muscles and the burning in her legs reminded her of just how much effort it had taken to get to that point, so dead animal be damned, she was going to figure out what was wrong with the 'Mech and take it for her own if that was even possible.

Stepping around the command couch, she gasped.

The woman sitting there looked like she'd been dead for no more than a few months, but, logically, Katie knew it had to have been decades. Her face looked gaunt and agonized. Her hair pulled back into a tight bun over the leathery skin stretched over the skull.

She had apparently mummified in her cooling vest on the command couch. There was a sizable hole in her shoulder, caved in. On her vest was a pin that might be some clue to the woman's identity, though Katie didn't recognize it. An inverted triangle with a black outline and a red field inside. Some sort of animal head, straight on and in black, stared forward in the center of the red.

Katie thought the woman was beautiful and haunting and was surprised at herself for being able to resist the urge to scream.

She'd never seen a dead body before.

"I'm so sorry," Katie told the mummified corpse. "I'll see you get a proper burial."

Katie vowed to bury the woman herself, fashioning a grave for her at the feet of the 'Mech. Since she had no idea who this woman was or where she'd come from and had no way of knowing where she'd *want* to be buried, that seemed like the most sensible option. Especially since leaving her in the 'Mech wasn't possible.

The 'Mech was Katie's now.

It was *her* 'Mech.

Katie smiled.

She had a 'Mech.

31 JULY 3143

"Where you goin' these days?" Scarecrow asked.

"Oh, nowhere," Katie said, doing her best impression of an innocent teenager.

"I see you leavin'. You're barely around. Unless there's a 'Mech to be worked on, you skedaddle right out of here. Everything okay?"

"Yeah, everything is fine. I'm just—wrapped up in my studies, I guess." She handed him a wrench for the joint motor assembly they were rebuilding in the center of his shop.

He took the wrench and narrowed his eyes. "You seein' a boy?"

"No."

"A girl, then?"

That made her blush. "No."

"Someone special at all?"

"No, Scarecrow."

"Feels like it's been months since we had a proper talk. You sure you're alright?"

"I'm fine. Better than fine, even. I promise."

Scarecrow smiled slyly. "Are you up to something?"

Katie did her best to suppress a smile. "Not... No. Not really."

Scarecrow went back to the work, which she watched carefully. There was more at stake for her to learn than ever. "Well, whatever it is you're doing, I hope you're bein' careful. I know I'm not much of a...well...a guardian or nothing, but I look at you like family, such as it is. I don't want nothin' happening to you."

Katie smiled. Genuinely. Honestly. Scarecrow was doing his best to reach out to her. To be there for her. But she still felt uneasy telling him about her little secret. "I know, Scarecrow."

"All right, then," he said, getting back into his work. "Just keep an eye out and learn what you can."

As she watched, she daydreamed about being able to go back into the jungle and work on her own 'Mech. She'd determined, to the best of her ability, that it was a *Kit Fox*. It was a Clan 'Mech, and she figured she knew how it got to Jerangle. One of the biggest clues about how the 'Mech had gotten here was the pin on the cooling vest. Apparently, the woman had been a member of the Kell Hounds, which was a mercenary unit Katie hadn't heard of, but now tried to read up on as best she could. How she got a Clan 'Mech away from the Clans in the first place was a mystery Katie wished to uncover. How she got to Jerangle, doubly so.

She was able to piece together how the 'Mech got left behind in this specific spot, though. There had been a record of a battle near Potsdam. A small one, but a battle nonetheless. The mentions were vague, but Katie's best guess was that the Kell Hounds were retreating, and the pilot had gotten stuck with an overheating 'Mech. She tried to stop by the river. Katie wondered if the pilot was going to try to dip in and cool her 'Mech that way, but she never made it. Stuck in the trees.

She'd been wounded; the cockpit had suffered a savage hit, and the radio was broken. She hadn't been able to call for help. The mysterious MechWarrior had cooked in the *Kit Fox*'s cockpit, waiting for help that would never come.

Katie did everything she could to give the woman a warrior's funeral. To honor her for her sacrifice. To honor her for everything she had given to Katie, even if she didn't know it in life.

Because that 'Mech was going to change Katie's life. It already had.

"Katie...?" Scarecrow said, interrupting her thoughts.

"Huh? What?"

"I said give me the spanning wrench and the spot welder, will you?"

"Oh," she said. "Right."

"You're sure nothing's wrong? You got your head in the stars again?"

"Something like that."

"More dreams of bein' in a BattleMech?"

Katie smiled. "Is it that obvious?"

"Katie, sometimes I think if you don't get behind the cockpit of a 'Mech, you're liable to explode."

"You're not wrong." And what he didn't know wouldn't hurt him. She was as close as she'd ever been to getting the 'Mech back to the shop.

She thought she'd surprise him with it.

She hadn't dared move it, though, because she hadn't figured out how to get it out. With no jump jets, getting out of the ravine would mean a dip in the river and she didn't know if the current would be too much for the 'Mech, or if the water would be too deep.

When she'd read about the Battle of Tukayyid, where the Prezno River had killed so many 'Mechs on its own, the last thing Katie wanted was to lose her 'Mech as soon as she had found it.

A low rumble shook her violently. Not just her, though: Scarecrow, the 'Mech joint assembly, and the whole shop.

"What in the hell is that?" Scarecrow asked, lifting up the goggles he'd been using to protect his eyes from the spot welder.

Katie shrugged. "I don't know."

The rumbling got louder.

And then there was the distinctive sound of laser fire.

"We're under attack," Scarecrow said matter-of-factly. He tossed the goggles and welder down and ran for the massive doors of the 'Mech shop.

Katie followed, surprised at how fast Scarecrow moved. She'd never seen him move *anywhere* that fast before. Possessed of some energy beyond him.

When Katie reached the doors, her eyes widened.

They *were* under attack.

It was a pair of 'Mechs, dirty and in disrepair, but functioning. They were painted black with red stripes. One looked like a barely-functioning *Crossbow* and the other an old battered *Sentinel.* Where they'd been dug up was anyone's guess. Probably from back in the time when the Lyrans had fought off some sort of attack on Jerangle or another. And the Lyrans had sported some 'Mechs that were already old even then.

She wondered how these pirates got them working. But they must not have been working very well. Both 'Mechs carried masked soldiers of some kind. They gesticulated with rifles and shouted wildly.

"What are they saying?" Scarecrow asked. His hearing wasn't as good as it used to be.

But she couldn't blame him. It was hard to hear *anyone* over the sound of a 'Mech tromping through a city street.

"It sounds like they're upset."

"I can see that."

Katie strained her ears, but still couldn't make out what they said any better than Scarecrow.

But when the *Crossbow* turned and punched the top of the bar, collapsing the roof in on itself.

"What the hell are they doing?" Scarecrow said.

"I hope you didn't need a drink today."

"Damn it."

Then, the *Sentinel* gestured with its right arm—the one that wasn't a cannon—and the MechWarrior inside (though Katie doubted he was a *real* MechWarrior) flipped on their external speakers. "Potsdam Town! We are the Red Stripe Raiders, and we declare you our subjects."

Scarecrow groaned. "These idiots are gonna get someone killed."

The *Sentinel* pilot carried on with their screed. "I have transmitted to you our demands. If the supplies we have asked for are not on the loading docks by tomorrow at sundown, we will tear this city apart."

For good measure, the *Crossbow* then kicked the building across the road from the bar. Katie couldn't quite see it. The 'Mechs were a couple streets away, and the only thing she could see were their torsos over the tops of the buildings.

With their threat transmitted and their timeline clear, they turned and left the town.

The idiots hanging on the tops of the 'Mechs, looking like they were ready to fall off anyway, hooted and hollered and fired their guns into the air.

It was an unmistakable show of force.

"What do we do now?" Katie asked.

Scarecrow shrugged.

Naturally, the whole town met in the municipal center. The mayor presided; a big woman with a fiery temperament and a last name she could never live down: Warhammer. Like the 'Mech.

Who had a name like Warhammer?

No wonder she kept winning elections in the town.

That, and no one really bothered running against her. Who wanted the job of administering a backwater town on a backwater planet?

It was a thankless job.

And now she had these so-called Red Stripes to deal with. They'd demanded money and crates of supplies. They must have a hovertruck of some kind to steal away with everything in addition to their rusty 'Mechs.

Scarecrow wondered out loud to Katie if, perhaps, they didn't have any ammo for their 'Mech's weapons, save for their lasers. The *Crossbow* should have had two mediums, and the *Sentinel* should have had a light one. But even those could have been stripped for parts a century prior, or sold for scrap at any point between then and now.

One of them had definitely fired a laser when they'd entered the town. That was what Katie and Scarecrow had heard that brought them out of the shop. Others had seen it. But beyond there, there was no guarantee that they had ammunition for anything else.

Mayor Warhammer stood at the front of the room, shushing the crowd. Her black skin served as a stark contrast to the white walls behind her. "Now we know what they've asked for, and I don't see as though we've got much of a choice but to give it to them."

"We don't have that many kroner," someone from the crowd said.

"Why would we turn them over, even if we did?" someone else shouted.

"But what else can we do?" came another voice.

Katie couldn't argue with any of their questions. But neither did she have any answers for them.

Mayor Warhammer didn't have answers for them, either. Despite her strength as a leader and as a person, she had no answers because the town was out of options. "Calm down, everyone," she said over the din of the townsfolk. "Settle. Settle down all of you. Settle."

But that didn't quite settle them down. A low roar of private conversation still filled the room.

That didn't stop the mayor from continuing. "We've been in tight spots before. And we've always come out on top. This whole world almost burned, and we're still here. Our grandparents and our great grandparents survived through the worst time in the history of our world, and we're not going to let a couple of jackasses with reclaimed BattleMechs threaten us or scare us away from what we need to do."

There was a modest cheer from the crowd.

"So," she continued, "I want ideas. I don't think we can just hand them our goods and our cash. But I'm also not sure we have a choice. The old defenses of the town aren't working, and we don't have anything but AgroMechs to field against them. Even if they only have one working laser between the two of them, they'd tear us apart and we'd lose even more."

The crowd murmured back and forth, some agreeing with the mayor, others dissenting. All of their voices, even in disagreement, still held respect for her.

"Anyone?" the mayor asked. "Does anyone have an idea?"

Katie did.

She raised her hand, sheepishly.

She wasn't sure she wanted to speak in front of such a large crowd. She wasn't always sure she wanted to speak in front of Scarecrow, let alone the entire town. This absolutely terrified her.

"You!" the mayor said, pointing a finger right at Katie. She made eye contact, and Katie almost withered beneath the mayor's gaze. For a moment, Katie forgot that she'd even asked to be recognized. Such was the power of a mayor named Warhammer.

Like the 'Mech.

That thought put a smile on Katie's face and she tried to speak in her loudest, bravest voice, though the results were mixed. "What if someone were able to chase them away...?"

The mayor laughed. "If someone could chase them away, I'd pay them half of the twenty-five thousand kroner these clowns are asking for."

Katie's eyes widened. "Seriously?"

"Absolutely. Now do you have any ideas for real? We know we want to chase them away."

"That's all I needed to know." And Katie turned, running from the room as fast as she could, leaving everyone to wonder what the hell all of that was about.

1 AUGUST 3143

The next day left the town of Potsdam in tense agony. As a collective, they'd decided they would pay the Red Stripes off for now, but they would also look for other means to destroy them in the future, even if that meant paying mercenaries. As it was, with communication across the Inner Sphere so slow, there was simply no time for them to come up with a better plan.

But they didn't know what Katie was up to, either.

She didn't want to tell anyone her plan until she was sure she'd be able to pull it off.

There were still so many unknown factors.

She'd spent the better part of two months fixing everything on the *Kit Fox* that she could. Every system relay, every bad batch of wiring. She'd even been able to patch a couple of pieces of armor with some sheets of metal small enough for her to carry out of the shop on her back. She'd brought more rope, too. And a rope ladder, so there had been less difficulty in getting down.

She did her best to keep the route hidden, though. And she didn't clear many of the trees in the copse that kept the BattleMech secret. She didn't want anyone to spot it like she did, if she could help it. Granted, no one had found it in maybe a hundred years, but once one person found it, the chances of another doing so skyrocketed.

She made a few last-minute checks of the repairs she made.

Katie was a good student, and Scarecrow had taught her well. Even if she'd never be a MechWarrior, she'd be a helluva 'Mech tech.

But why not both?

Settling into the command couch with the cockpit hatch closed and sealed behind her, it was time for the moment of truth.

Strapping the cooling vest—sans the aged company insignia—and settling the neurohelmet on her head, she was ready to go.

She placed her hands on the controls and started the ignition sequence. The old 'Mech hummed with power. "Okay, *Kagekitsune*," she told the 'Mech, "we're going to do this."

As if responding to her words, the console flashed to life, a constellation of lights and readouts.

A chill traveled up Katie's back and a tear rolled down her eye when the viewscreen came to life.

She'd never seen anything more beautiful.

The sun was still high in the sky, but falling fast. Dusk approached and she was running out of time and she hadn't even gone anywhere yet. She still had to get the 'Mech to Potsdam.

She hoped this would be the most difficult part of her day.

Taking a deep breath, she put her finger on the firing stud on the control stick, hoping one of the weapons worked. She'd not been able to test the integrity of any of the weapons, even the lasers, because she hadn't wanted to draw attention to her 'Mech. But now, she had no choice. And she wasn't going to make it out of the shadows if she didn't blow her way through the trees.

She hit the stud, but the only thing she heard was a horrible clicking.

Must be the short-range missiles, and I'm out of ammo.

On some level, she was relieved. The last thing she would have wanted was to cause an explosion of missiles that close to her 'Mech. Maybe she needed to do a little more research before she just started pushing buttons.

But there wasn't time.

Katie pulled the trigger on the control stick and her screen flashed a brilliant shade of green as the medium lasers fired, incinerating the trees before her in an instant.

Maybe she could have just stepped through the trees, but this seemed better somehow.

Before her stood only the river.

You can do this. You can do this. You can do this.

She repeated the mantra in her head as she willed the 'Mech forward for its first step. It wobbled a bit as it cleared the freshly-lasered tree stumps, but its chicken leg held firmly on the shore's bank. One more step, and she'd be walking into the river.

She'd studied the water depth on maps in the library, and found that it never got deeper than two or three meters. And the flow of water was brisk, but not insurmountable.

If the 'Mech held together and the walking was relatively even, she assured herself that she would be okay.

You're really good at lying to yourself, though.

Another deep breath, and then she moved forward into the drink.

The *Kit Fox* didn't so much step into the water, but hopped.

Katie thought that would be a better way to deal with the height discrepancy between the ledge of the river and the river itself. With her external mics on, she took in the sound of the rushing water. It changed in tone when the 'Mech changed the pattern of the water. It got louder, too. Maybe one of the mics was on the legs?

She took slow steps through the water, hoping she would be able to keep her balance and not drown in her 'Mech.

She smiled.

It didn't matter though.

She had a 'Mech.

And it worked.

She was going to be a MechWarrior.

She just had one last thing to do.

Mayor Marjorie Warhammer stood at the edge of town, watching the sunlight slowly dwindle during its golden hour, along with the chances of saving her village from the so-called Red Stripe gang.

These fools had cobbled together a couple of old 'Mechs and thought that was enough to scare the entire town. And, well, they were right.

As much as they wanted to resist, they simply didn't have the means.

No amount of pitchforks and threshers would stand up to the Red Stripe 'Mechs, no matter how righteous they felt their cause was. And no amount of strapping small arms on an AgroMech would help either. Again, their righteous fury meant nothing. There was a feeling unique to humanity that if people felt their cause was just, they would win no matter what the odds were. Since the dawn of humanity, they had told each other stories about good triumphing over evil and it made a lot of people make a lot of bad decisions.

Not that good shouldn't triumph over evil.

In the final accounting, it usually did.

But a lot of good people got killed going up against impossible odds because of that fire in their belly.

And the good Mayor of Potsdam didn't want to see that happen to any of the good people in her care.

Potsdam had been through a lot over the years, and she didn't want to see it go through any more hardship. The people around those parts were good, and they deserved some easy times, though since the war and the bombs, easy times seemed harder and harder. They were resilient, though. And as difficult as it was, they'd weather the Red Stripe gang, too, as frustrating as they were.

She wondered if it was some of the local kids who had found the 'Mechs, but then she realized how absurd that would be. None of the local kids had the know-how to repair a salvaged 'Mech, and these kids had a bit of a different accent. Maybe they were striking out on their own from one of the other close settlements. Arnhem, perhaps. Or even all the way from the capital of Snowy Monara, though that seemed like an incredibly far distance to raid a small town for a pittance of kroner and supplies.

As the sun dwindled further and the light turned from gold to gray, the mayor sighed.

The sound of the 'Mechs approaching came like thunder, a deep booming bass you could feel when they walked, right in the pit of your stomach.

It was something the mayor hadn't felt in a long time before these clowns showed up.

And she hoped it would be a long time still before she heard it ever again after their exchange.

The mayor walked down to the loading docks herself. It was just a staircase down from the rooftop lookout she'd chosen to watch the sunset from. She'd oversee the handoff personally. She didn't want to risk anyone else's life. And besides, she knew everyone in town. If she could make the handoff herself and they got close enough to do it, she might be close enough to recognize who they were and what they were up to.

The *Crossbow* and the *Sentinel* with the sloppy paint jobs and Red Stripe goons hanging off of them like they were a children's jungle gym sauntered toward the town's loading docks. Behind them was a hovertruck, just like the mayor had guessed would be there.

The mayor felt the rumble of each step of the two 'Mechs and it became more and more pronounced as they got closer.

On top of the crates of supplies they'd demanded, foodstuffs and medicine and technological components, was a bullhorn for the mayor's use.

She lifted it to her lips and spoke, "Red Stripes. This is Marjorie Warhammer, the mayor of Potsdam. We have everything you asked for. And a case full of kroner, in cash, since you weren't able to provide an account for transfer."

Mayor Warhammer raised the suitcase full of kroner to accentuate her point. She'd hoped they'd just give her an account number and they'd be able to trace these people that way. It would have been a lot easier to recover the money, even if the banks were dodgy themselves.

"We hope you'll take this and leave. Our business will be concluded, and we'll all go our separate ways."

The Red Stripe 'Mechs stood sentry on either side of the street as the hovertruck backed into the loading docks, ready to take their booty.

They didn't say anything, but they were going to have to come face to face with her to get the case full of cash. She wasn't going to just let them take it.

The driver and passenger of the hovertruck hopped out and approached. Maybe they'd gotten better uniforms since last she saw them, or knew they had to wear them more properly because they were going to be in closer contact with people, but both of them wore greasy-looking black jumpsuits that had a stripe of red painted along the front. It was as sloppy as the paint job on the *Crossbow* and the *Sentinel.* By the look of the stiffness of their fabric, Marjorie would have wagered it was even the same paint.

Real amateurs.

They wore masks that obscured most of their faces. Goggles and helmets hid the rest. They were taking no chances with their identities being exposed. And the mayor wasn't the best with voices, so she wondered if she *would* be able to recognize them at all.

"Give us the case," the driver said in a gruff tone that confirmed the mayor's suspicions. Indeed, she could not recognize the voices.

"Are you sure you want to do this?" the mayor asked, hoping that by getting them to talk more, she might get more clues about their identity.

"Of course we are. Now hand over the case and no one gets hurt."

The voice sounded gruff, but not terribly gendered one way or the other. Still not enough information.

The mayor tightened her grip on the handle of the luggage and hoped beyond hope things wouldn't be this easy for them.

And then her brow furrowed.

The vibration of a 'Mech moving rumbled through her feet and into her body, but neither the *Crossbow* nor the *Sentinel* were moving.

Both of the Red Stripe goons looked around, apparently wondering what could be going on, just like her. They seemed as surprised as the mayor was when they realized their friendly 'Mechs weren't moving either.

"What the...?" the driver said.

That's when the mayor saw it.

With the red paint and the mottled green moss covering over most of it, the old *Kit Fox* looked like something out of an ancient Christmas celebration. Part tree, part 'Mech.

Warhammer hadn't seen a 'Mech like that...well...ever.

Something about it told her it wasn't one of the Red Stripes though. Part of it was that the paint scheme didn't match. And as ignorant as these Red Stripe fools were, they at least had a dedication to their matching uniforms and paint schemes.

The other major part was that the *Crossbow* and the *Sentinel* both scrambled to get into a position to get the *Kit Fox* in their firing arc, all but ignoring the mayor and the promise of their loot.

There wasn't time for them to do much, though.

The mysterious *Kit Fox* opened fire with its green lasers, and blasted right into the *Crossbow*'s torso with a direct hit. The lasers carved off a massive chunk of the *Crossbow*'s middle, proving that the thing was weak enough to begin with, barely held together. The bandits hanging onto the *Crossbow*, not wishing to experience close laser fire a second time, leaped off the 'Mech as its ruined torso armor panel *clanged* to the ground.

Those had hadn't injured themselves ran for cover, the others limped or crawled away.

Mayor Warhammer wanted to cheer at the mystery 'Mech drawing first blood. But she worried the *Kit Fox* didn't look much better and it was outmatched, two to one.

The *Crossbow* was able to twist around in and fire back at the *Kit Fox,* melting a fragment of its leg armor, but not before taking another laser hit that cut off one of its arms, sending it crashing to the ground.

For the *Sentinel*'s part, instead of firing back, it charged the *Kit Fox*, spilling its own riders along the way. Unfortunately, it couldn't close the distance in time.

The *Kit Fox* backed up and opened fire with a deafening double blast from its Ultra autocannon.

The *Sentinel* crashed into the ground, skidding on the pavement in front of the *Kit Fox.*

The mysterious MechWarrior that had come to the rescue of Potsdam aimed their lasers down at the *Sentinel* and fired them once more into the top of it, blowing a hole into it.

But that gave the *Crossbow* enough time to fire another blast at the *Kit Fox.*

Its first shot flew wide, blasting into the trees beyond it in the outskirts of town. The mayor hoped it didn't start a fire in the forest. That was the last thing she needed to deal with on a day like this.

The second shot hit the *Kit Fox* in the nose of its cockpit. The 'Mech was already mostly cockpit, a big, mean shell with spindly arms and raptor legs. Warhammer knew it was known for having weak armor in the head, and she worried that the mysterious benefactor wouldn't make it through this.

The *Kit Fox* took another step back and repositioned itself so that the *Crossbow* was back in its firing arc and fired again. Both lasers turned the center of the *Crossbow* into slag and it fell over.

The hovertruck driver and his passenger looked on in horror.

Then they turned back to the mayor, who only smiled at them. She dropped the case full of old C-bills and pulled a pistol from her hip, aiming at both of them.

The pistol didn't threaten them enough, though. They both ran, scrambling to get into the hovertruck, despite being empty handed. They didn't want to lose their lives any more than they wanted to lose their 'Mechs. But it had happened anyway.

The mayor fired a shot, but it flew wide.

The Red Stripe goons were able to get into the hovertruck, back it up, and attempt a reckless J-turn to straighten back out and escape.

The *Kit Fox* didn't seem to like that. It marched around the downed *Sentinel* and aimed its lasers down at the oncoming hovertruck.

It fired.

The lasers blew a hole in the road in front of the truck, and an explosion of dust and debris clouded much of the mayor's view. The hovertruck must have swerved to miss the pit, because the next thing she heard was a great crash.

The Red Stripes had collided into the building to their left. The pirates piled out of their wrecked vehicle and looked as though they were going to try to run, but the *Kit Fox* side stepped again to keep them in its firing arc.

Then, its external speakers flared to life.

"Red Stripe pirates," the voice said. It was the voice of a young woman straining to sound gruffer—and perhaps older—than she was. "Surrender or you will be destroyed."

Both of them cowered beneath the withering stare of the *Kit Fox,* their hands raised, granting the MechWarrior's wish. The rest of the bandits that had fallen or leaped off the two destroyed 'Mechs also raised their hands.

The mayor jogged toward them, leaving the bullhorn, but taking the case full of cash and the gun. She was going to arrest these fools herself and detain them with the help of the *Kit Fox* until the sheriff of Potsdam arrived to throw these clowns into the lockup.

"Hold it right there," she told them, leveling the pistol at them.

"We surrender, we surrender!" they said, flinching at the thought of being shot.

It was amazing what being robbed of your firepower and 'Mechs would do to the bravery of a person. It would reduce it right down to zero. These fools had nothing left and no power with which to bargain.

Only after the sheriff had arrived and hauled all the bandits off did the *Kit Fox* finally stand down.

"MechWarrior!" the mayor called up to the old 'Mech. "I'd like to thank you."

"Thanks aren't exactly necessary," the 'Mech pilot said through their external speaker, though they must have realized it was far too loud to hold a conversation that way. Unless they were trying to *remain* mysterious, there wouldn't be any problem with them getting out of their 'Mech and talking to the mayor one-to-one.

And that's exactly what happened.

The hatch on the back of the *Kit Fox* swung open and, just as the mayor had predicted, a young woman climbed out. She still couldn't quite tell who it was or if she knew the young woman, as her back was turned while she scaled down the side of the 'Mech.

"I think thanks *are* necessary. You saved our town."

When the MechWarrior spun around, the mayor was shocked to find that it was Scarecrow's grease monkey, Katie.

Katie Ferraro...? Yeah, that's it. She must not be older than sixteen or seventeen, tops.

"I mean, thanks are great and all, but I think there was something else." Katie had grease smeared on one cheek and her old and tattered cooling vest looked like it had been taken out of a museum.

"Something else?"

"You told me that if I could take care of these guys, I'd be able to get half of the money they asked for. So, I still think that's a pretty sweet deal." She looked around the street at the damage she had wrought and her eyes widened. Maybe she didn't realize how much destruction she could cause in a 'Mech when viewed from ground level. "Wow... I would, uh, also like to salvage their 'Mechs that I took down."

All things considered, Mayor Warhammer thought that would be a pretty good deal for the town. *Then Katie would be responsible for cleaning up the salvage* and *the street.*

She smiled. "I don't see why that would be a problem."

Katie toed the ground in front of her. Clearly there was something else on her mind.

"Was there something else?"

"Well, maybe, I was thinking…"

"Out with it, young lady."

"Well, I was thinking, what if you needed the services of a 'Mech to protect the town on an ongoing basis."

"You mean a contract?"

"Yeah, like a contract."

"That's something we could talk about, MechWarrior."

When the mayor referred to Katie as a MechWarrior, she saw the girl's eyes go wide and a blush come across her face as she smiled.

That was it.

She wants to be a MechWarrior.

Mayor Marjorie Warhammer returned the girl's smile.

A MechWarrior she will be…

CROSSBOW
HEAVY—65 TONS

KIT FOX (ULLER)
LIGHT—30 TONS

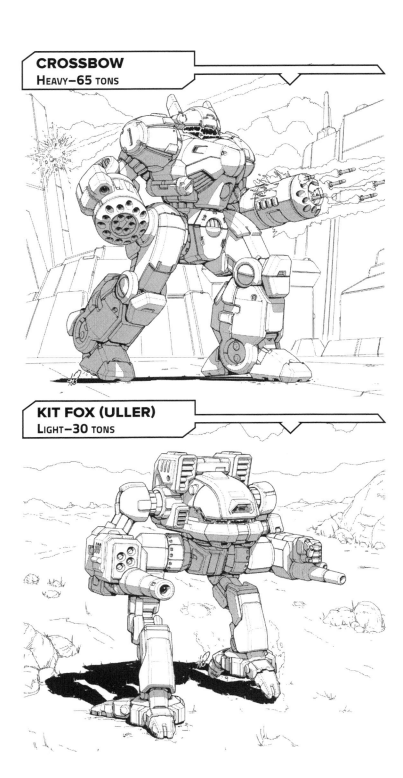

TWO
THE FOX PATROL

"Anything on your scopes?" Katie Ferraro asked her subordinates over the radio as she moved *Kagekitsune,* her *Kit Fox,* slowly around the dark perimeter of Gothenburg City. It was weird, ordering around a couple of adults way older than her, but she had founded the Fox Patrol and they were grateful for the work. A merc unit was the natural result of a teenager finding an abandoned 'Mech in Jerangle's backwater and having the skills to fix it up themself. At least that's what Katie told herself while edging around the soaking farmland on the outskirts of the ninth largest city on Jerangle and trying to act older than her nineteen years implied.

"Nothing here," Evan Huxley said. He did his sentry duty in a *Locust,* painted in the standard Fox Patrol colors of rust red and gray, running in wider circles around the city than Katie had, owing to its speed. Gothenburg was arranged in a circle, with four main quadrants and the old town in the center. It was the biggest city Katie had ever seen, but she knew that was because she hadn't been much farther than her old home of Potsdam. Stretching from the edges of the city were farms to the east and west and rice paddies to the north, where they were more easily flooded by the river. As big as Katie found it, it was a quiet place, doubly so when everyone was on edge about another raid at any second.

"Quiet as a tomb on this front," Arkee Colorado said. He was Evan's boyfriend—the two of them came as a pair—and he piloted the heaviest 'Mech in the Fox Patrol: an ancient *Quickdraw* that had seen more battles than they would ever know. The two were both in their early twenties, though Katie never talked about age with them. Seemed like it would only cause her problems. To their credit, though, they never flinched at taking an order from her. At least not on account of her youth.

On one hand, Katie didn't like hearing it was quiet. Things went bad when the situation was quiet, and it had been a week of quiet nights. On the other, hand, they were being paid to protect Gothenburg from a trio of mercenaries calling themselves the Jerangle Raiders. True to their name, they'd been running night raids against the city. Gothenburg had a problem, and no one else could help them. The Fox Patrol had been hired to deal with the Raiders. If there was no problem, Katie's unit was still getting paid their retainer.

The profit margin of the Fox Patrol was razor thin. If they had a particularly damaging engagement, they might even end up losing on the deal. But Katie knew what she was getting into. The Jerangle Raiders were minor players. Ill-equipped. Their 'Mechs were barely armed, since ammunition was so hard to get on a remote planet like Jerangle.

One day, we'll get to fly away from this place.

"Wait," Arkee said. "I've got something weak coming through here."

"What is it?" Katie asked.

"I think it's a 'Mech. It's coming up hot on my scopes. Nothing around these parts that hot at all unless it's a 'Mech, right?"

"Probably." Katie wondered what the best course of action would be. If a 'Mech barreled toward them on the other side of Gothenburg, beyond the mid-rises, and she and Evan both came over to back Arkee up, that would leave the rest of the city exposed. As far as they'd been able to gather, the Jerangle Raiders only had three operable 'Mechs, so racing to fight one 'Mech would be a bad idea. "You think you can handle it?"

"Listen, Captain, I think I can handle anything."

"I don't need bravado, Sergeant. I want an honest answer."

"I don't even know what it is. Wait…"

The radio dropped, and a flash of light brightened the sky across the city. Then, a moment later, she picked up the sound of the explosion.

"Arkee? What's happening?"

Katie zoomed out her radar display, hoping she'd be able to catch something—anything—of the situation Arkee found himself in.

"Orders, sir?" Evan asked through clearly clenched teeth. She knew he must be stressing. That was his best friend under attack.

"Do you have anything on your readouts?"

"Nothing, sir. But it sounds like he's in trouble. I'd really like to help."

Katie took in a breath and held it, wondering what she was going to do if it was a trap. "Do it. Move fast, stay far away. Scout the situation. Jump in if you can actually help, but if he's gone, we can't afford to lose you, too."

"Affirmative, Cap'n."

For Katie's part, she would bide her time. She would make sure there wasn't a second 'Mech waiting in the wings to leap out and finish raiding the city. The Jerangle Raiders were already upset enough that the denizens of Gothenburg had refused to give them protection money, but the city had also hired the Fox Patrol for *actual* protection duty. Katie could just imagine the leader of the Raiders wondering how Gothenburg had been able to afford mercenaries.

He must have been pretty pissed off.

The Fox Patrol was doing everything they could to keep him from raiding any more towns or villages in the sleepy ruins of Jerangle.

Evan didn't say anything over the radio for a full minute. Another flash in the distance told Katie that *something* had happened.

"Arkee? Evan?" Glancing at her HUD and all of her other dials and displays, she tried gleaning anything she could about the situation. "What's going on down there?"

She scanned the area ahead of her, beyond the outskirts of Gothenburg, making sure she had no enemy signals of her own. When the readouts all came out clear, she began making a wide circle with her *Kit Fox* around the perimeter again.

Since she'd been able to slowly learn how to acquire the ammunition for her short-range missile launcher and was able to get both lasers working again, she was finally able to use her 'Mech like it had been designed. *Kit Fox*es were perfect for hammering foes at long range, and then coming in close for the kill. Her large laser would serve the farthest out, then, when she had the ammo, the missiles and autocannon would help finish the job at short range.

In the absence of information in the Jerangle night, she wasn't sure if she'd be seeing anything at *any* range for her to shoot at.

"I've got eyes on him, Cap." That was Evan's voice.

"Why isn't Arkee talking?"

"Unknown. He's not responding to me, either. But I'm not seeing anything else on the scopes or on visual."

"Where the hell is he then?"

"Looks like he got hit. Pretty good, too."

That's just great. How much are we going to sink into replacing his 'Mech components if he's hit that bad? she wanted to say, but didn't. "Is he okay?"

"Unknown." She could hear the worry in Evan's voice.

"I'm on my way." Katie willed the *Kit Fox* to move faster, coming close to its top speed as it sped around the perimeter of the city.

Katie hated cutting through cities. She was always convinced that she'd knock a building over and didn't want to be liable for it. That was the last thing she could afford, though with Arkee's life on the line, she was tempted.

But Evan was there.

He could take care of Arkee if she couldn't. She was just the backup.

They were smart.

And she was glad she'd found them.

Arkee and Evan had come as a package deal. Had sought her out, actually. They were a two-man merc unit, and they had just gotten so far into debt they couldn't fix their 'Mechs. She was able to bring them on to the Fox Patrol for a song, and in return she just had to keep the jobs coming in and their 'Mechs purring like kittens. Or foxes. Whichever. That was the advantage of her training to fix 'Mechs since she was just a kid, an advantage she figured she'd have in commanding a 'Mech unit.

She liked them and didn't want to lose them.

She got the impression they wouldn't have many other places to go anyway. For whatever reason, they found a home with Katie and the Fox Patrol, and she found she spent as much time fixing the 'Mechs as she did finding jobs.

Maybe being in charge was actually the worst idea because it yielded the most responsibility. The two boys could just go off and play while she had to see to the contracts and make the payroll and afford the repairs and then effect them herself.

Katie sighed. She'd grown up too fast, and they were content to let her.

"Evan, talk to me."

"There's no 'Mech around, and he's still out of communication. Maybe he got hit and his radio went dead?"

"Not likely. And if that's what happened, what were those lights in the sky and the bogey on his scope?"

"Fair."

"Maybe they're jamming him," Katie said.

"That seems unaffordable to an outfit this ragtag."

"Fair."

Katie had almost made it around the bend, doing her best to keep an eye out for any other bogies as well as listen for any other signs of hostile activity.

The radio crackled. "—do you copy?"

"Arkee?" Katie said.

"Captain, it's Arkee."

"What the hell happened?"

"Hit-and-run attack. Knocked me down and knocked me out. Blacked out for a minute."

"You okay?" Evan asked. Naturally, that was his primary concern.

"I think I am, but my *Quickdraw* is going to need some help. I've got damage on my torso and shoulders. Lost some armor. I think they were aiming for my missiles, maybe they'd hoped I'd just explode?"

"Great." Katie gritted her teeth.

If they were going to have a showdown, they'd need to fix the *Quickdraw* fast. And she didn't know where she'd get any replacement armor. Maybe she'd just have to weld sheet metal on the damn thing. Maybe Mayor Becker would know of something she could use and deduct it from their pay.

Or maybe Arkee went out into battle having taken the hit and he just needed to be careful.

"Aside from the armor, you're functional, though?"

"I think so."

"Good. It's going to be dawn soon, and the patrol will be over. I can start work on repairs."

"Affirmative."

The damage to Arkee's *Quickdraw* was superficial, but that didn't make it any less obnoxious to repair.

Gothenburg's municipal officials had given them a warehouse deep in the dirty industrial district on the south end of town as their base of operations. Grimy with rust and soot, it was tall enough to admit their 'Mechs, which was more than could be said for most of the other buildings in town. The warehouse hadn't been outfitted with much, but the Fox Patrol had their own repair kit, and that included the scaffolding Katie would use to fix the heavy 'Mech. She stood high up on it, assessing the damage while Evan and Arkee stood close to each other below, looking up at her while she worked.

They both had their arms folded.

"You know, you two could help," she said.

"You know I'm useless with repairs. I'm a MechWarrior, not a 'Mech tech." Evan said with no hint of guilt or sarcasm in his voice.

"I know, I know." He really *was* terrible with repairs. All thumbs. It was actually spectacular how much worse he made things when he tried to help. "What about you, Arkee? You're the one who did all of this damage. Can you help?"

"I'm worse than him, and you know it. Don't like heights, either."

She shook her head.

What in the world was she going to do with these two?

They needed to score a job big enough that they'd be able to hire some techs and she wouldn't have to do all of this herself.

At this rate, she was already giving up sleep in order to work on the 'Mechs. If she couldn't get them to take less damage or if she couldn't find easier jobs, they were going to simply drown in repair costs. They wouldn't last long as a merc unit long enough to develop the reputation she wanted.

So she doubled her efforts and worked even harder.

She thought about what Scarecrow—the man who had trained her and adopted her after her parents died—would say. His voice echoed in her ear as though he were there: "*Just take it one task at a time. Break it down as best you can and just chew on the little bits. Soon enough, you'll be crossin' things off your list left and right, and then the 'Mech'll be done. In the blink of an eye.*"

She missed him.

It was hard enough losing her parents. Losing Scarecrow was like losing her folks all over again. He'd been so delighted when she brought home the *Kit Fox*, and he'd showed her how to fix it and tune it up in ways that had still been beyond her. He had done everything he could to pass on what he knew before he died, but cancer got him. That's what happened when you lived in one of the irradiated zones of the planet for an extended period of time. He hadn't made it to Potsdam soon enough, and then it just went downhill from there.

It wasn't fair.

She couldn't believe she'd only had the 'Mech for a little more than two years, and she'd lost Scarecrow right in the middle of that. It all felt like a different lifetime. A life she mourned as much as her parents, biological and adopted alike. She wished Evan and Arkee could have met him. They'd have liked him.

But, like she approached the BattleMechs she repaired, so too would she approach her grief. One small task at a time.

"Could you at least bring me the tools I need?" she called down to Evan and Arkee.

But they were already gone.

She had to remind herself that she liked them and they were great MechWarriors and even good company. Because otherwise she was going to scream.

Wasn't she the captain?

After all, they had given themselves their titles. They'd all heard that the most storied merc units all had military ranks in their hierarchy and the captain was typically at the top, so since Katie seemed to know what she was doing, Evan and Arkee had decided that title should go to her.

Katie climbed down the scaffolding to collect the tools she needed, dreaming about what life would be like if she was an *actual* merc. Instead, she felt like all she'd done was play one. Like when she used to play MechWarrior as a kid, pretending to stomp around and actually pilot a 'Mech.

Mayor Becker had some scrap he could send over for her to make the *Quickdraw* structurally sound again. The repairs weren't going to be that bad.

And, like Scarecrow had always said: the sooner she got to work, the sooner she'd be finished.

It took six hours after the mayor's delivery before the *Quickdraw* was in enough fighting shape that it wouldn't be at any significant disadvantage if they had to run and fight. And after a night of patrol and then all those repairs, Katie needed to sleep.

Time in her bunk was precious.

They'd converted the warehouse's offices into sleeping quarters. It wasn't an elaborate setup, but it was the best they could do. It wasn't like they could afford other accommodations, and this came free with the gig, so she couldn't complain.

She blacked out the windows and did her best to crash.

Katie closed her eyes and felt like she'd only barely just blinked when there came a knock at the door.

"Wha...?" she said.

Why would someone be knocking on the door while she was sleeping?

"Is everything okay?"

The mystery person knocked on the door harder, as if in response to her question.

"Fine, fine." Katie blundered toward the door in the dark and unlocked it. As she opened it, the a sliver of blinding sunlight expanded and filled the room.

"What is it?" Through squinted, bleary eyes, she saw Arkee. He was the bigger of the two, and bearded. His jumpsuit was rust red, like all of their Fox Patrol gear.

"We just got a message."

"So?"

"It's from the Jerangle Raiders."

She was able to open her eyes a little bit more. "*What*?"

"They sent us a challenge."

"A challenge? Who do they think we are? The Jade Falcons?"

Arkee handed her a noteputer with the message on it, and when she got a look at it, she wondered if the Raiders really did think her outfit was a Clan of some sort.

"It's a challenge," she said, reading over it.

"That's what I said."

"They want us to meet them. They say they've only got three 'Mechs and want to meet the three of us on 'the field of battle.' At sundown."

"That's what it said."

"Jesus."

"Yup. What do you want to do?"

"I don't know. Should we do it? What if it's a trap?"

Arkee shrugged his shoulders. "I mean, don't we go into everything thinking it's a trap?"

"Generally." She handed him back the noteputer and then rubbed the sleep from her eyes. "How long was I out?"

"Few hours."

"How long till sundown?"

"Few hours."

"You're really helpful, Arkee, you know that?"

"I do my best."

"Where's Evan?"

"Sleeping still."

"Wake him up. We've got a lot of prep to do if we're going to be ready to meet them. But first, I'll let them know we accept their challenge."

"We do?"

"Yeah. We're going to have to fight them anyway, right? They knocked you out last night and ran. You didn't even see them."

"But I did see them."

"Okay, what 'Mech were they piloting?"

Arkee looked down, avoiding her gaze.

He'd forgotten, if he'd even looked. And he almost certainly hadn't checked his 'Mech's battleROM recording to go back and learn anything, like she had.

"It was a *Marauder*," Katie said. "We're going to lose this slowly, or we're going to come out on top all at once. The Raiders don't realize it, but they just gave us the means to do it. We'll figure this out. We're smarter than them. We're better MechWarriors than they are. Even you, Arkee. They're sneak-attacking us because they know we have them dead to rights."

"Then it's a trap."

"I think so, yeah. They want to meet in the rice fields. That's a lot of wet and soggy land our 'Mechs can get caught in. And the Raiders know our fight may ruin this whole crop of rice, putting Gothenburg in an even worse position this year. To the point where maybe they'd be unable to afford keeping us on the payroll come harvest time."

"So we tell them to take a hike?"

"No. We spring the trap."

Arkee's face fell, and his eyes narrowed with suspicion. "That sounds like an absolutely terrible idea."

"Listen, if we know it's a trap, we'll be ready for them."

"But what trap are they springing? Is it just the battlefield? Do they have more 'Mechs than we do? Artillery? Infantry hiding in the rice fields? How do we know?"

"We don't. But we'll do our best."

"I mean, that's fine with me. It's your call. You're going to be the one fixing the 'Mechs."

"If we survive."

"You're not exactly inspiring me with confidence."

"Send them a note back. Tell them we accept."

"You're insane."

"I'm not. It'll work out."

"Are you sure?"

"Yes. Just go. Do it."

"If you insist." Arkee left, exasperated. He was more annoyed than she'd have liked him to be. She wanted him to be gung ho about the plan. She just needed to figure out exactly what that plan was.

She glanced at her chronometer and realized she didn't have much time to figure it out.

As they approached the appointed rice fields for their challenge, Katie was sure she had a foolproof plan.

The Fox Patrol would play to the strengths of each of their 'Mechs. She would stay as far away from the center of conflict as possible, maximizing the damage she could do from long range until it was apparent she'd be able to close in and help make the kills.

Arkee would stay in a medium range and do his best to soak up damage and deal it to the best of his ability. His 'Mech was the heaviest and could take the most abuse, despite what the engagement the night previous had indicated. In a fight with opponents he expected, he would do okay.

Evan though, he was the secret weapon.

*Locust*s were some of the fastest 'Mechs ever built, but they were vulnerable. A couple of good hits and they were toast. It was really an awful 'Mech to round out their trio, to be honest, but they went to battle with the 'Mechs they had, not the 'Mechs they wanted. Evan had salvaged the *Locust* and done the best he could with it. Or at least tried to, which is why he needed Katie. But Evan would take his 'Mech and race through the battle, adding confusion with lightning-fast hit-and-run attacks.

Sure, the rice fields might be a little tricky for him to maneuver, but the rice and the water were bigger problems when the 'Mechs were standing still. Running along would work just fine. As long as he didn't get stuck in a fight, he could strafe them with his lasers and keep moving.

Aside from the *Marauder* she had seen on Arkee's battleROM footage, Katie didn't know exactly what assortment of 'Mechs they would be up against, but in her experience, the sorts of 'Mechs operated by bandits on Jerangle weren't as well maintained as the 'Mechs of the Fox Patrol.

For Katie, that was the secret. A well-maintained 'Mech would always perform better than the usual scrap they saw around here.

Still, she couldn't help but be afraid of what the Raiders could field in this skirmish. For them to issue the challenge, they had to feel they had some upper hand. And they had knocked Arkee's *Quickdraw* to the ground pretty quick.

"You two locked in and ready?" she asked over the radio.

"Affirmative, Cap'n," Evan said.

"Locked and loaded, Cap," Arkee said.

"Be sure to stick to our formation. It's going to be hard enough to navigate this as it is, I don't need you two clowns breaking the formation or the plan. We've got one good chance at this."

"Sometimes," Evan said, his voice full of happy charm, "one good chance is all you need."

"Sounds like an on old Kurita proverb," Arkee said.

"More like a fortune cookie," Katie said.

Evan was having none of it, though. "You really think a Kurita could be as pleasant or charming as I am?"

Katie rolled her eyes. "Let's cut the chatter and focus on the task at hand."

She really needed to work on their discipline. If they were going to be a genuine fighting unit with some sort of quasi-military cohesion indicative of a first-rate mercenary unit, they'd have cut down on the wisecracks over their closed channels.

What would someone listening in think?

It could turn into a nightmare.

In fact, on sleepless nights, one of her recurring nightmares was exactly that: being disrespected by other MechWarriors.

Evan and Arkee had kept silent, so they must have listened to her well enough.

"You in position, Evan?" she asked. He should have been. He had the closest distance to travel and the fastest 'Mech among them.

"Yessiree." His cheer was pleasant enough when they were just hanging out. She could see why Arkee was attracted to him. He was very easy to be around. But on what could be a death march, it was just a little too much for her taste.

"Good." She checked for any sign of the opposing 'Mechs and still couldn't see anything. "And Arkee, you're almost in place?"

"Almost."

"You picking them up?"

"Nothing yet.

"When you catch a blip, send over your telemetry and scan data."

"Affirmative, Cap'n."

It wasn't a minute longer before the bottom dropped out of the operation.

"Oh, man, you're not going to like this, Captain."

Arkee only ever pronounced all the syllables when it was trouble.

"What is it?"

"Looks like three heavies. Sending information now."

Three heavies? "That's just great."

By the time she got the data, she could see the enemy 'Mechs standing as specks on the horizon. Her computer had already tagged them. The lead 'Mech was a *Marauder.* Standing behind them was a *Catapult* and a *Galahad.* Katie suddenly wondered how much of her plan was in jeopardy.

Unless the winds blew in their direction in just the right way and every hit they made was lucky, they were going to have a hell of a time.

There was no way one heavy 'Mech and two lights stood a chance against three heavies unless *everything* went their way.

Katie saw only the most narrow path to victory.

The *Catapult* was equipped with enough long-range missiles and lasers to bury all of them on its own. And the *Galahad* was a menace with not one, but *two* Gauss rifles. The *Marauder* boasted PPCs, lasers, and autocannons.

None of this was going to be pleasant.

Maybe I should call a retreat.

"Orders, Captain?" Arkee asked.

He was the one out there in the front, his 'Mech ankle deep in the reflective pools of the rice paddies. Waiting for them to arrive.

How do we play this?

"Patch me through to your externals."

"Got it. Say the word and you're hot."

"Go ahead." Katie paused for a second, gathering her thoughts. "Jerangle Raiders. This is Captain Katie Ferraro, leader of the Fox Patrol. The city of Gothenburg is under our protection. We have come to meet you to hear your demands. Understand that we parley from a position of strength. Your 'Mechs do not intimidate us. Transmit your demands now and we will discuss further."

She flipped the channel so only her compatriots could hear her. "Well, we'll see how they respond to that."

She wondered how the local farmers, living in the sparse houses around the edges of the rice paddies would react to hearing the threat. Would they be scared of collateral damage or ruined crops? Or would they feel confident that the Fox Patrol would save them?

As she waited for a response from the Jerangle Raiders, Katie hoped they would feel the latter.

But the waiting went longer, and she catalogued the clouds in the mottled sky and the dwindling sunlight.

Katie's stomach twisted into a pretzel. Every second that ticked by, the knot tightened.

What are they waiting for?

Were they speaking among themselves?

Waiting for the time to strike?

Would their response come in the form of a salvo of missiles aimed right at Arkee?

Suddenly, she didn't trust her plan all that much. And she realized Arkee had no business following her into battle anywhere.

"Damn it," she said into the radio.

"No cause for alarm yet." But Arkee's voice had a quiver of fear in it.

"Easy for you to say. You're the one out there flapping in the wind for all to see."

"Hey, I agreed to this plan."

"You said, and I quote, 'This plan is terrible.'"

"Yeah, but just because a plan is terrible doesn't mean it's the worst option we've got. I think this is just a big show of force, and we'll be just fine."

"Love, those are three heavy 'Mechs," Evan said. "We are *not* negotiating from a position of strength here."

"Maybe they aren't either," Katie said. But she didn't believe it.

"How long do we give them to respond?" Arkee asked.

It was a fair question. Katie glanced down to her chronometer on the console. Almost two full minutes had elapsed. That must have been one hell of a conference they were having among themselves.

"Have they moved at all?" Katie squinted at the 'Mechs on her viewscreen, then zoomed in to get a better look at them. All painted in a swampy jungle camouflage. "I can't even tell if they've moved."

"Not for a tick," Arkee said. "Best believe I've been watching them right close."

"Hmmm."

Katie found herself at a loss. There wasn't much she could do. The way she saw it, she had two options. First, she could wait for a response. Maybe this would all work itself out somehow without any more fighting. Maybe it wouldn't. Second, the Fox Patrol could simply begin their attack.

The Raiders certainly wouldn't be expecting it. They had the bigger, better 'Mechs. They had the choice of battlefield. They had all the cards.

But, maybe, with the element of surprise, the Fox Patrol could focus in on one and get the drop on them.

Katie exhaled deeply.

She didn't enjoy making these decisions, but she was the best person for the job. Evan and Arkee were much better at following orders than giving them. Still, she wanted everything to be very clear. Chess was not a game she often had the patience to play. She found herself making moves faster and faster until she heard someone say "Check."

That was an impulse she would have to work on.

Recognizing that, she took in a deep breath. "We'll wait. But I can't imagine what's taking them so long."

"Copy that, Cap'n," Arkee said.

And that brought a smile to her face. If he was calling her "Cap'n" again, then he'd cooled off just a bit. Or at least the stress wasn't eating him so bad.

"Hold on there," Arkee said. "Wait just a second."

But she saw it, too.

The *Marauder*, mean and menacing up front, aimed its particle projector cannon right at Arkee. It looked like there was going to be a fight after all.

The PPC blasted Arkee, its bright light reflecting off the water of the rice field, making it look even brighter than normal.

Watching her readouts, Katie hoped Arkee would make it through okay. That patch job on his torso wasn't the best she'd ever done. It was a rush job through and through.

When the shot flew wide, she smiled. Her adrenaline spiked, and the rush of it coursed through her.

"Do it, boys! Fire at will! Focus in on the *Marauder* and stick to the plan!"

"*Affirmative*!" they both called out.

And that was that. The decision was made for her. Time for her to get into range and start blasting.

She wasn't far.

Katie locked in on the *Marauder* and fired her large laser. She could take potshots at the 'Mech all day and stay far enough way to be largely out of range of the Raider pilot's worst attacks.

Her lance of laser energy cut a thick chunk of torso armor from the 'Mech.

Arkee opened fire just as quick, his *Quickdraw* launching a salvo of long-range missiles. They peppered the *Marauder* across its entire body; some hit the legs, some the torso, some the cockpit itself. Chunks of armor blasted away from the 'Mech, and Katie had to do a double take to be sure. "That *Marauder* seems a lot softer than it looks."

"Copy that," Arkee said.

"I'm incoming," Evan said. And from the left side of her view screen, she saw him there, a speedy spec of a BattleMech, racing across the rice fields. His aged *Locust* looked like a pair of rust-red streaks, as his reflection doubled in the still water of the paddies.

He lashed out with his medium lasers as soon as he found himself in range, ablating much of the armor on the *Marauder*'s right arm.

The *Marauder* pilot showed great discipline in keeping its target locked in on Arkee. It pulled back, behind the *Catapult* and *Galahad*, and planted its feet in the water while firing its medium lasers.

Arkee took the hit in the torso, right over the patched armor.

"Arkee?" Katie shouted. The last thing she wanted was to lose her biggest 'Mech right at the beginning of the conflict.

Evan closed the distance between him and the *Marauder* by half and unleashed another barrage of lasers that lacerated the 'Mech's arm once more.

Katie fired her large laser again and furrowed her brow as it struck the *Marauder* squarely in the leg. "Wait... What are the other two 'Mechs doing? They haven't moved whatsoever."

"They haven't fired a shot, either," Arkee said.

"What's their game?" Evan asked. Something was definitely wrong. MechWarriors didn't just fall asleep at the switch like that. They should have been firing hell itself at them. By all rights, Arkee should have been toast instead of lightly toasted by a single PPC hit.

The *Marauder* opened fire again, and its PPC smashed through most of the *Quickdraw*'s torso.

"You okay, Arkee?"

"Can't take many more hits like that. But where are the other two 'Mechs?"

As far as Katie could tell, they hadn't moved a single centimeter the entire time. Zooming her visual sensors for a closer look on them, they looked barely able to stand. Most of their joints had been fused or damaged. The *Catapult*'s missile racks were empty. The ends of the *Galahad*'s Gauss-rifle arms were even sawed off and rusted.

"It's a ruse," she said.

"Come again?" Evan replied.

"Think about it. We come out here, we see three heavies and decide to negotiate with them because we're not suicidal. It's a bluff. The *Marauder's* the only target right now. The other two are statues. It's just a con. They're empty shells with warm engines to make 'em look like targets."

"But what's the point?"

"A show of force. Only fools would attack a force that looked like that."

"I resemble that remark," Evan said, taking mock offense.

"She's right, though, Ev," Arkee said.

"Of course I'm right. Now hammer that *Marauder* and we'll be done with it."

"What if the other two are playing possum, though?" Evan asked.

It was an intriguing possibility, but Katie had her doubts. "Even if they were just out of ammo and acting as a screen, they could still do a lot of damage in a physical fight. They're just there to look scary."

But then her heart skipped a beat.

If they made it out of their jam, that *Catapult* and *Galahad* would make some great salvage. If they were anything close to workable, they would make the Fox Patrol able to punch a lot harder for their size.

Katie had to stop herself from daydreaming further as she circled back around to other possibilities.

She fired on the *Marauder* again, as did Arkee. Evan zoomed by once more, taking one last potshot. It was enough to take the *Marauder* down. The cockpit armor wasn't sound, and their shots were able to crack it open like an egg, dribbling steel all down the front. The *Marauder* crashed backward, and it put a smile on Katie's face.

They were going to come out of this okay.

And she was doubly glad she'd made Mayor Becker put a salvage clause in their contract.

"So, I guess that's it then," Evan said, bringing his 'Mech to a halt at the feet of the smoking wreckage of the *Marauder.*

"I guess," Katie said. "That was a lot easier than I thought it would be."

"Me too," Arkee said. "I'll be honest, I thought I was a goner."

"Do me a favor and knock those other two 'Mechs over, would you, just in case? Having them standing up and staring at us is just freaking me out."

"Affirmative, Cap'n." Arkee moved in and tried pushing over the *Galahad.* It didn't fall, though. "You ever just try to knock a 'Mech over, Cap? It's not as easy as you'd think."

"Do whatever you need to. Just make sure it's out of commission. I don't want to risk anything."

Indeed, something still set her teeth on edge. A creeping fear in her stomach crawled up to meet the panic in her chest. Something was wrong.

"There's big tire tracks all over the place here," Arkee said. "Deep ruts in the mud. The Raiders must have just drove these suckers in on flatbeds since they can't move on their own."

"Good to know, but that means something is up." She turned on her frequency scanner, going through as much of the unencrypted civilian frequencies as she could find. The radio squelched and screeched as it scanned until it stopped on a channel and she heard what sounded like a scream.

"What?" she said to herself.

Then she waited for the situation to make itself known on the radio.

"It's an attack!" came a voice.

"Where are they?" came another. "How many are there?"

"They're on the south side! The industrial area."

"Three of them."

"Damn it." Katie had heard all she needed to. She clicked her radio over to the Fox Patrol frequency as she started circling her 'Mech around to head back into Gothenburg. "Fox Patrol, this was all a ruse to lead us out of town. They're attacking the south side as we speak."

"Damn it," Arkee and Evan both said.

"We need to get in there as fast as we can. If we lose too much of the city or the skirmish, we're not going to be able to keep any of this salvage, and that would make me unhappy. And you wouldn't like me when I'm unhappy."

"Sure thing, Cap'n."

"Evan, go scout ahead. See what we're up against. You'll get there first anyhow. I wonder how long ago the attack started."

She wanted to scream. This was not how things were supposed to go.

The Fox Patrol was a group of professionals. They didn't leave their flank—or their client—undefended. If they didn't turn this around fast, she worried it could be a black mark on their reputations forever. No one would ever hire them again.

"Arkee, you're the slowest and farthest. You'll just have to be the cavalry."

"I don't think I've got a choice."

"Likely not. But we can still win this, right? Early chatter on the city channels sounds like it's just three 'Mechs. We're good at range. Urban fights aren't so bad. The industrial section is mostly built high, but we can use that to our advantage. Hit and run. It sounds like a mix of weight classes. And as long as it's not three more heavies, I have every confidence in us."

"Don't jinx it, Cap'n."

"I would never."

Katie pushed her beloved *Kit Fox* even harder, wishing she could squeeze any more speed out of it at all, but it was already sprinting as fast as she could make it.

The heat in her cockpit was almost unbearable. Those laser shots threw her heat way up, and the forced march didn't help. She was grateful that her fighting uniform wasn't much more than a bathing suit and a cooling vest. If she had to be stifled by any more cloth, she'd scream about that, too.

Looking at the readouts, she wasn't going to be able to do much more if she didn't want to overheat. And there was nothing worse than a 'Mech frozen in the heat. Only amateurs pulled that sort of stunt. Though, she had to admit there were probably some 'Mech pilots who ran really close to the edge and would no doubt shut their 'Mechs down to win a battle if it were close.

She was a fine 'Mech pilot, but she wasn't that good.

Not yet.

And if she didn't get to the conflict soon, she was never going to be a MechWarrior of that quality.

Navigating through the streets of Gothenburg inside her treasured *Kagekitsune*, Katie felt like a stranger. She'd never been here before taking the assignment, and she didn't know it like she did Potsdam. And this city was so much bigger. It was big enough that it had parks and fountains and museums, which were all things she'd only assumed cities had. Katie figured she'd feel like a stranger in any town she found herself defending.

Feeling like a stranger didn't mean she wouldn't fight and die for them if need be. That was the life of a mercenary. Of a MechWarrior. Of a person who made their money piloting 'Mechs for a living. Like bodyguards or samurai or anyone else in history willing to take bullets for others in exchange for cold, hard currency, she was just the latest in that long line.

Katie would die for the people of Gothenburg if she needed to.

Though she hoped she didn't.

Evan saw them first and reported in. "I've got visual."

"What are we looking at?"

"Looks like they're emptying a warehouse. There's some light infantry sorts loading up trucks. As for 'Mech resistance, we've got three. They're in a *v*-formation, but it looks like they're on different streets. Two are close to your location."

"Models?"

"Looks like we've got two *Commando*s, and those are on your side, and what my computer is telling me is an old *Night Hawk*. All light 'Mechs, all painted in that same terrible Jerangle Raiders camouflage. "

"They're all old. Sounds like they're even uglier."

"Yeah, they're old, but that *Night Hawk* is ancient."

"Where did they even get this stuff?"

"We can wonder about that later, right?"

"If you insist."

"You're the captain, Captain. Should I engage? Or wait?"

"Engage on my mark. I want a visual of my own before we commit."

Three light 'Mechs. That was certainly promising. They had a fighting chance, even if their heavy was a good five minutes out. If they could use the streets to their advantage, it was possible.

Those *Commando*s could be vicious, though. They were light, but standing up to their lasers and missiles wasn't going to be easy. She would try to keep them at range, where their weapons would be ineffective and she'd be able to hit back, but the streets in the industrial district might not cooperate. Having two of them there doubled the threat. Her computer readout told her the *Night Hawk* was all laser-based. That meant they weren't going to run out of ammo. At best, they would just overheat when the time came. But 'Mechs that light and limber, she didn't see it happening in this engagement. If they fired enough to overheat, Katie Ferraro and her Fox Patrol were going to have far bigger problems than that.

She saw the boxy backs of the *Commando*s, and slowed to a stop. They were chasing down the city's own defenders, who were firing at them with small arms. Sure, they were light 'Mechs, but not even pistol and rifle bullets were going to faze them.

Katie could only imagine how pissed the locals were at having to defend their city. What the hell did they pay the Fox Patrol for otherwise?

Beyond them and a few streets over stood the *Night Hawk*. That must have been where the infantry were loading their trucks. The *Commando*s were the sentries sent to harass while the *Night Hawk* did the guarding.

None of the Raiders' 'Mechs seemed to notice Evan's *Locust.* It was a shorter 'Mech and a little more difficult to see over the buildings. And the Raiders must have had their attention on something else entirely.

That was good news for the Fox Patrol.

"Evan, we're going to go in hard and focus on the *Commando*s. The *Night Hawk* looks like it's busy, but if its buddies are in trouble, it may break off. We don't want to harass all three until Arkee gets here."

"I'm a-coming, I'm a-coming," Arkee said.

"What's your ETA?"

"Still a few minutes out. This *Quickdraw* isn't made for sprinting like you two are."

"Just get here as soon as you can. Evan, you take a hard turn and get the *Commando*s and rush them head on. I'll see if

I can flank them on the cross street. We'll pin them from two directions in the intersection."

"Sounds good to me."

"Let's do it."

Katie took a deep breath.

Using her console display, she tracked the distance between Evan's *Locust* and the *Commando*s, wanting to make absolutely sure the timing lined up to catch them in the crossfire. This would be the easiest way to deal with them.

Doing the calculus of speed in her head, she charged forward as soon as the *Locust* crossed that imaginary line, and put one of the *Commando*s within range of her lasers.

She fired, but the shots went wide, crossing in between both of the *Commando*s and sailing down the street until they hit the side of a nearby building.

The rear *Commando* definitely noticed her. It turned to face her while its compatriot faced off against Evan's *Locust.* It was going to be a showdown. The only advantage she had was she could hit the *Commando* from farther away, meaning she had some time before it could close the distance and be in range to shoot back.

Evan wouldn't be so lucky. He had to get in close, hit, and run.

As the *Commando* charged her, Katie thought to back up. If she could keep her edge of range and reach for even a minute longer, it would help her in the long run. But she moved backward a lot more slowly than the *Commando* charged.

Still out of range, the Raider shot their laser, but missed by a wide margin.

Katie fired her large laser, taking care to aim more meticulously. The reticule turned gold over the *Commando* and she fired.

The shot hit the right side of the torso.

Damaged as the 'Mech was, it didn't stop.

That thing is a lot better armored than it looks for a light 'Mech.

It dawned on Katie why the *Commando* charged her so quickly. It was trying to ram her. She supposed the idea was for the laser and missiles to melt the hardest pieces of her armor off, and at that speed, it would just bowl her over like a tenpin.

If she didn't put it down before it closed the distance, she was a goner.

Backing up, she wished she could increase her speed, but moving backward in the *Kit Fox* was already a pain. And slow.

But all she had to do was buy herself time.

Just a little extra.

The *Commando* closed the gap even farther and fired its laser again. She wondered if it even had ammo for its SRM launchers. Even if the *Commando* would have been in range, the shot missed, flying wide from the *Kit Fox*, much to Katie's relief.

"Come on, go down you bastard."

She fired her large laser again, but the shot missed.

"Damn it!"

Hopefully Evan was faring better against his *Commando*, but somehow she doubted it. They both had to get in the same range. He was definitely faster than the *Commando*, but if the Raider hit him with their laser a few times and rammed him good, it would be all over for the little *Locust.*

She prayed Arkee would get here soon.

The *Commando* managed to get a shot off that hit her. The bulk of her 'Mech was torso, and that's where the laser hit. Not enough to put her down, but enough to be threatening. Her indicators lit up, flashing from green to yellow.

Then she hit the firing stud and felt the heat rise in her 'Mech as both of her lasers lanced toward the *Commando* in a flash. The medium laser went wide, and the large laser hit the same arm, searing it off at the elbow joint.

The only thing she could do was back up more and try to sidestep the 'Mech if it got close enough to ram her. But, being in the *Kit Fox*, her limited mobility didn't lend to such a risky maneuver. She was going to have to put it down before it reached her.

But with how fast it charged, she wasn't sure she'd get the chance.

The *Commando* fired again, its laser missing her.

The heat rose and sweat poured from Katie's brow.

There wasn't any choice.

She triggered both lasers again and hoped their piercing coherent light would end the fight once and for all.

The *Commando* bucked under the damage as the lasers sheared off the left side of its arm and torso.

Its front armor melted right off. She'd cracked the egg open. All she had to do was make the kill.

Though its momentum slowed, the *Commando* staggered and kept coming at her.

She hit it with the large laser, turning the center mass of its torso structure into slag. Keeping its momentum, the 'Mech tipped over and skidded forward on the ferrocrete street. It came to a halt right in front of her.

Katie exhaled. She felt like she hadn't taken a breath in minutes, but she could finally breathe again.

There was no time to stop and celebrate, though. "Evan, do you copy? What's your situation?"

She tried to get a visual on the street where Evan's *Locust* was battling the other Jerangle Raiders *Commando.* Hopefully the one he dealt with was softer than the one she had taken care of.

"Evan? Do you copy?"

Then, through strained breath and a patchy radio signal, he spoke. "Little busy..."

She spotted smoke rising from a building on the cross street, but couldn't see the either of the 'Mechs. Had they both gone down? They could have been obscured by any number of taller buildings.

The only thing she could do was keep moving. She couldn't help if she wasn't there.

"Arkee," she called out, "What's your ETA?"

"I'm close."

"Define close."

"I'm coming."

Damn it.

They were all going to be slag before he got there.

Katie pushed *Kagekitsune* up the street as she double-checked the instrument panel and her damage gauge. Her midsection—which was effectively her entire cockpit—flashed yellow. As did the left arm.

She could take another few hits, but it wouldn't be good for her.

Then she checked her heat scale. The exertion of walking wasn't helping the heat come down very fast, but her 'Mech *was* cooling. She shouldn't have pushed the lasers so hard, but what other choice did she have?

That Jerangle Raider would've been the one left standing if she hadn't pushed the heat. And they would be the one turning around to help *their* friend out of the jam they were in. No, she had made the right choice.

She'd decided she was going to be a MechWarrior at the age of nine, and back then she'd never realized that being a MechWarrior would involve so many life-or-death decisions.

Every battle was life or death.

And she had to force herself to remember that.

Rounding the corner, she had to take a wide arc.

That was the only thing she hated about her trusty 'Mech. She loved it. She loved the story of it. She loved the feel of it.

She loved everything but how hard it was to turn.

When she lined up at the street, the scene before her wasn't anything like she expected.

The *Commando* had crashed into a building and toppled over. That was the smoke, coming from the rubble and the resultant fire. Evan's *Locust* was crouched down, aiming its weapons right at the *Commando*. Since the *Locust* was closer to Katie than the *Commando* wreckage, she assumed the *Commando* had gone in to charge and missed. When it crashed, Evan must have circled back around to knock it out completely.

"Evan, you done?"

"I just wanted to make sure they didn't get back up."

"They're not. We've got more work to do."

"Affirmative, Cap."

The *Locust* ceased its assault and turned around to face Katie. "What's the plan?"

Katie brought Arkee back into the conversation. "What's your ETA?"

"Almost there."

She wished she could do something about the speed of his 'Mech. It didn't seem likely. Mass had as much to do with his speed as anything, and his 'Mech was 60 tons; they didn't classify it as a heavy for no reason.

"So, here's what I got," Katie said. "We take it from both sides."

"That's your plan?" Evan said. "We take it from both sides?"

"I mean, do you have something better?"

"Not... I mean... No. But that doesn't change the fact that we just—"

"Listen, Evan. We're in big stompy 'Mechs that go pew pew. Are there many more plans than just picking an angle and shooting at other big stompy 'Mechs from that vantage point?"

"Well, I..."

"Not really. Yeah, there's a lot of strategy in picking that vantage point, but we're fighting in the streets. And that *Night Hawk* is right in the middle of the street. There's really two options for 'Mechs like ours without jump jets. We take it together from one side, or we corner it from both sides. No, we don't have a whole lot of options for plans. At least hitting it from both sides gives us a way to cut it off and force it to work harder to pick a target. Now I'm the captain here, and if you want to second-guess my orders, you just go ahead and do it, Evan. But I'm the captain, God damn it. And I'm doing my best to keep us all alive and fed and in 'Mechs that work. Do you have a problem with that?"

"Er, well, no."

"Then listen to me."

"Captain..." Evan's 'Mech backed up, aiming its gun right at her.

"What did I just say?"

"No, Captain, you don't get it."

And then suddenly she did.

The *Night Hawk*. Behind her.

Just rounding the corner at the edges of her viewscreen.

"Damn it, Evan! Shoot them!"

Katie negotiated her *Kit Fox* to start making that slow turn so she'd be able to get the *Night Hawk* in her firing arc.

You really just love opening your mouth for nice, long diatribes only to put your big metal 'Mech feet inside of it, don't you, Ferraro?

Her viewscreen flashed green with the *Locust*'s laser hits. And Evan unloaded with his machine guns, too. Just for good measure. For all the good they'd do against the *Night Hawk*.

They were more meant for infantry.

And Katie didn't think he realized how expensive ammo for them was. Otherwise he'd have stuck to just his lasers.

No sense in arguing about it now.

That was what had got them in this part of the predicament in the first place.

Seeing a target in profile must have been too good for the *Night Hawk* to pass up. It tore into Katie's *Kit Fox* with its entire complement of lasers.

On her console's damage readout, her right arm flashed from green, to yellow, to red. The armor melted right off, exposing the inner workings of her 'Mech.

Katie continued her turn, hoping she'd be able to get the Raider into her firing arc before he destroyed her completely. "Evan, keep the pressure on."

"I'm doing everything I can." He changed directions, moving forward. He was going to strafe the *Night Hawk* on his way by. It was as good a plan as any since they—no, *she*—had botched their chance at catching this clown with their pants down.

"Do more. Just a little more," she said, working as fast as she could to get the *Night Hawk* in her sights.

By the time she came around, a barrage of missiles struck the *Night Hawk*'s torso. They exploded around the pod-like cockpit and rent chunks of armor right off.

"Arkee!" she cried, delighted.

Evan blasted the *Night Hawk* once more with his lasers, and they seared right into the cockpit, punching through before she even got a chance to fire.

Arkee appeared down the street in his *Quickdraw,* looming over the smaller 'Mechs like the shadow of a skyscraper.

"Nice of you to show up," Evan said.

"Well, I couldn't let you both take all the glory."

"Glory?" Katie said. "This was more of a mess than anything. There are 'Mech parts everywhere. And I think the people of Gothenburg are going to be pissed we let the city take as much damage as it did."

From the periphery of her viewscreen, she could still see the smoldering rubble around the *Commando* Evan had defeated quite successfully.

"Well, we'll see about that, won't we?" Arkee said.

Katie wished they'd been paid up front so they could just sneak out of the back of the city and never talk about any of this again. Maybe Mayor Becker and the people of Gothenburg could just forget the Fox Patrol had ever been there.

She took a deep breath, mortified.

How was she going to spin all of this?

Katie smiled, feeling like a fool for having worried.

Things could have gone a lot worse, but they went so well. Better than she could have ever hoped.

The people of Gothenburg assembled a first-rate celebration for them. The town hall was decorated in the Fox Patrol's colors, and the city's mayor, Reif Becker, a short, skinny man with a tangle of gray hair, gave a toast in front of all the city to hear. "We owe you dearly, Fox Patrol!"

The crowd erupted in shouts of "*Hear, hear*!"

They all raised mugs of ale and swayed and shouted, honoring their guests on the dais.

Katie and crew wore their cleanest mechanic's coveralls, as much the uniform of the Fox Patrol as anything.

"You've saved us from the Jerangle Raiders," Becker continued, waving his mug back and forth. "And you saved our city in the process!"

Katie felt uncomfortable, drinking the cityfolk's beer and accepting their cheers while their mayor spoke like he was in some cheap movie.

But if they wanted to celebrate the Fox Patrol, she wasn't going to stop them.

At the end of the toast, Arkee and Evan, arm in arm, turned to kiss each other jubilantly, and the crowd cheered even louder.

But Katie started doing the calculations in her head, and the sounds of the party dimmed in her mind. Since the Fox Patrol would be able to take all of the Jerangle Raiders' salvage, she'd be able to scrape together at least two or three more functioning—barely—BattleMechs to add to their forces.

But they would have no MechWarriors to pilot them. And with the time it would take her to repair all six 'Mechs, factoring in room and board and storage, she, Evan, and Arkee would be lucky if they could leave Gothenburg at all.

Maybe they'd be trapped here forever, looking for the next job that would give them enough of a down payment to send them to the next place.

Katie chewed her lip.

Evan, a bright smile on his face, wrapped his arm around her and took another long draught of his beer. "What do you look so concerned about, Cap?"

"I have no idea how we're going to survive on these margins, Evan."

Arkee wrapped his arm around her from the other side and smiled. "Don't worry, Cap'n. We'll find a way."

"I hope so, boys." She looked out at all of those smiling faces in the crowd and hoped they'd tell the story far and wide. Maybe they'd get something good out of all of this. "I hope so."

COMMANDO
Light—25 tons

CATAPULT
Heavy—65 tons

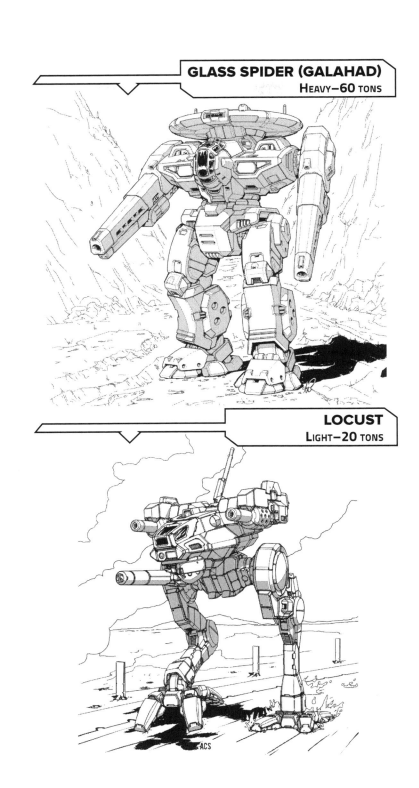

GLASS SPIDER (GALAHAD)
HEAVY—**60** TONS

LOCUST
LIGHT—**20** TONS

MARAUDER
HEAVY—75 TONS

NIGHT HAWK
LIGHT—35 TONS

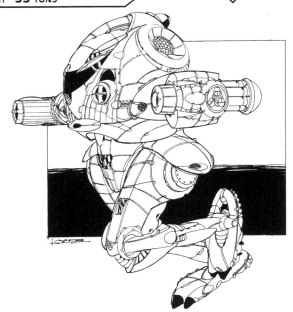

QUICKDRAW
HEAVY—60 TONS

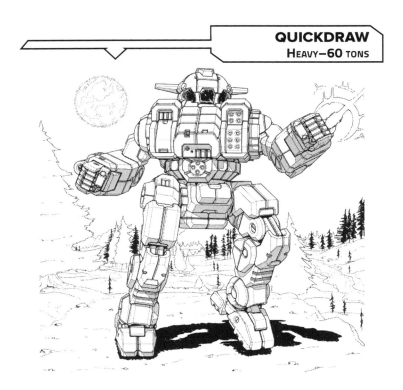

THREE
THE FOX AND THE BEAR

MUNICH
JERANGLE
LYRAN COMMONWEALTH
13 AUGUST 3148

"Lordy, would you look at this?" Katie Ferraro said, eyeing the old DropShip from the edge of the landing platforms. An ancient, modified *Confederate* class, it was in rough shape, but still spheroid, for the most part, and a steal.

It was also the exclusive new DropShip of the Fox Patrol. And they'd done it a lot faster than they expected. They'd saved up for it for three full years, but had expected to save up for ten. The seller said it was hot, but Katie chose to believe that was a euphemism for something else. Nothing would dampen her spirits, no matter how mangled the ship was or sketchy its circumstances were.

We've finally done it, somehow. A place of our own. A place to call home base without having to move from city to city, warehouse to warehouse.

And no more being stuck on Jerangle. Katie knew they could now take bigger and better jobs across the galaxy.

"I don't think this thing is flyable," Evan Huxley said. "And even if it is, it's definitely not safe." A wiry 'Mech-jock of a man, he was a third of the original Fox Patrol.

Evan's boyfriend, Arkee Colorado, was a much bigger man, with a thick beard of tight, black coils. He was the final third of that first lineup of the merc unit. He stood behind Katie and Evan and gawked at the ship with the same wonder and disgust. "I think you're losing your mind if you think we're going to make that thing spaceworthy."

"It *is* spaceworthy." Katie was adamant. She would not have them impugning the honor of their new ship. It was going to take them to the stars and beyond and into the real world of high-profile mercenary work. They'd done everything they could on such a dead world.

"You're joking, right?" Arkee said.

They approached the spaceport together, walking like a merry band of three.

"We'll have to fly it if we're going to get to our next contract."

"Wait," Evan said, "they committed?"

Katie nodded. "I signed this morning."

Evan couldn't hide his excitement. "Yes!"

Arkee had always been the more realistic of the two. "And they're paying us to go all the way to Kaesong in *that* thing?"

"Looks like. They stipulated the travel bonus and everything."

"Jeez. There is truly no rest for the wicked, is there, Cap'n?"

"No, Arkee. No there isn't."

When they arrived at the *Fox Den*, Dexter Nicks and Rhiannon Ramirez, the newest MechWarriors, were already there. Along with Frankie Fischer, the pilot and mechanic Katie had found. She was so thrilled that she'd finally found someone she trusted to pilot the DropShip *and* work on the 'Mechs. It had been so exhausting being the only one in the unit who could repair their babies. Adding tech work to her leadership role made it a complete and colossal pain in the ass. But Frankie was great. They were everything Katie wanted in a wrench-monkey: resourceful, easy to get along with, competent. Mainly it was competence she was excited for. And they didn't joke around much either, which made them a welcome relief from Evan and Arkee's constant faux-bickering and wisecracks. In a lot of ways, Frankie reminded her of Scarecrow. And maybe that was the most important thing of all.

She missed him.

Dexter and Rhiannon had already loaded their 'Mechs into the DropShip. Katie and the boys still needed to bring theirs from the warehouse to the *Fox Den.*

Frankie was there, too—older than Katie, to be certain, but not by much. What was a decade between fellow mechanics? Frankie wore loose-fitting maintenance coveralls in the soon-to-be-classic Fox Patrol rust-brown color. It made their frame completely androgynous, and that matched the sharp angles of their face and their close crop of buzzed hair. They walked around with a noteputer, doing last minute checks and maintenance to keep the ship spaceworthy.

"Any major problems, Frankie?" Katie asked.

"It *looks* like a piece of junk," Frankie said, "but it's got everything we need. This'll be just fine. And a song for what you paid for it. You sure it's not hot?"

"Worry about that later. What do you still need to get us to Kaesong?"

"I'll hire some contract pilots to fill out the crew, I can't do that all myself. And we've got a couple systems that need some wiring touch-ups, but other than that, I think we're good to go. I've already got our cache of spare parts loaded up. If you finish up with *Kagekitsune* and Sergeants Colorado and Huxley bring their 'Mechs in, we should be ready to shove off tomorrow or the day after, at the latest."

Katie smiled.

"Sergeants," she said to Evan and Arkee, doing her best to respect the quasi-military decorum of the little mercenary unit she'd spent so long building, "go retrieve your 'Mechs from the warehouse and do a final sweep. Make sure we didn't leave anything important behind. *Fox Den* is our home now. Treat it as such."

"Aye, aye, Cap'n," Arkee said.

"Affirmative, Cap," Evan said.

"Hop to it, men."

And they left, taking with them the palpable excitement she knew they felt. They were just as excited as she was that they had a semipermanent place to hang their spurs. The three of them had been through so much together. They'd gone on jobs where they had to sleep in the mud and hide from enemy infantry. They'd bunked up in the dodgiest warehouses in the dodgiest parts of the dodgiest towns that remained even half-thriving since the bio-attacks generations ago had shriveled so much of the planet's ecosystem.

They'd seen war and peace and feast and famine.

She smiled, watching them walk out of the *Fox Den*'s loading dock together. They were finally going to get off Jerangle.

Once and for all.

CONFEDERATE-CLASS DROPSHIP *FOX DEN*
VANGELIS CITY
KAESONG
RASALHAGUE DOMINION
16 DECEMBER 3148

Katie looked out the bridge windows as the *Fox Den* turned toward the planet and began its descent toward Vangelis City.

She'd never seen anything so beautiful.

The aurora of light as the DropShip entered the atmosphere danced along the reinforced glass and reflected in her bright brown eyes.

Wondrous.

That was the only word she could use to describe it.

She'd never been off Jerangle. And here she was, the second planet she'd ever set foot on.

Turbulence rocked the bridge and sent Katie's heart into her stomach. *Second planet I will* hopefully *set foot on.*

"Everything okay, Frankie?"

"Everything is great, Captain," Frankie said. They sat behind the command console and capably kept all the hired deckhands in line. "We're all set. Just a little chop on the drop, that's all."

The screech of twisting metal did not fill Katie with confidence, but if Frankie wasn't worried, there was no reason for her to worry either.

"You seeing this?" she asked, though to no one in particular.

Frankie and the hired crew were the only people on the bridge. The MechWarriors were all resting as best they could. She imagined Evan and Arkee would be in each other's arms, getting the most out of their private room together in what very well could have been their last few minutes alive.

They weren't nearly as optimistic about the construction of the *Fox Den* as she was. When they attached to the JumpShip, an awful reverberation through the whole DropShip sounded like wind rushing through a hole in the vacuum, and they'd both freaked out.

Understandably.

Ramirez and Nicks hadn't said much. They'd only been on a few missions with the Fox Patrol, and hadn't really ingrained themselves into the group yet. It was hard to just join a small outfit that had been around awhile without feeling a little bit like an outcast.

Watching Kaesong grow closer and closer, she wondered how she could make them feel more included. She didn't want anyone to feel the loneliness she'd felt in the time between losing Scarecrow and finding Evan and Arkee.

The DropShip rocked violently, and Katie gripped the armrests of the chair she was buckled into. "You sure everything's all right, Frank?"

"We're doing good, Captain. Trust me. Everything is good."

But Katie had seen the outside of the ship. She knew Frankie could have been exaggerating just to put her at ease. But she could have sworn a piece of hull plating on the giant ball of a ship had come off.

The commander of the Fox Patrol took a deep breath and did her best to stay calm. *Everything is fine. It's all fine. None of us are going to die a horrible death, crashing into the atmosphere of a strange planet while our 'Mechs are stored uselessly in the hull.*

Nope. That isn't how it's going to go at all.

Katie tried calming her nerves over the rapid descent, but finally she just had to close her eyes and hold on.

A DropShip was nothing like a 'Mech, and she didn't want die in a ship she wasn't piloting herself.

Faith in Frankie and their hired crew was all she had, and it would have to be enough.

For all of the stress, the landing was smooth, and they reached the surface of Kaesong just fine. Vangelis City wasn't the biggest city on the planet, but it was big enough that they needed help from the Fox Patrol. The DropShip's blast pit sat at the end of a ferrocrete landing strip that stood on the outskirts of town. And in the contract she'd negotiated, she was able to get the landing and parking fees waived so they could use the *Fox Den* as, well, their den, without incurring further costs.

Their employer would pay when the job was done, but this job would be easy. The free-room-and-board concession seemed to make sense, though it had taken the last of the Fox Patrol's reserves to buy the DropShip and hire a JumpShip that would take them to Kaesong.

They'd had to move quick, though. JumpShips around Jerangle were about as rare as anything in that region of space. Especially since the planet had been so far out of the way for so long that it didn't receive many visitors. Most would never bother to visit and see that people were living quite imaginative lives struggling to survive there.

And Kaesong was a long way away. They'd had to travel through Jade Falcon territory and into the Rasalhague Dominion. Katie was grateful the route hadn't proved treacherous. Jerangle was a nowhere planet, and Kaesong likely didn't matter in the grand scheme of things, either. She just wouldn't mention that to those she did business with.

"We're safe and sound on the ground, Captain Ferraro," Frankie said as they powered down the DropShip. Engines whined as they came to a halt, and the hum of the ship slowly dissipated.

"It's going to be wonderful to be back on the ground," Katie said.

"We *are* on the ground."

"I mean, like with my actual feet."

"Oh, right. I understand."

"Send the word that we'll be meeting in the conference room to go over the mission in one hour."

"Yes, sir."

Frankie went to work as ordered, and Katie began rehearsing her big speech.

The conference room had windows on one side. Normally, they would look out into the glory of space, but now they looked over Vangelis City. It was a beautiful urban area, the largest Katie had ever seen. A half-dozen skyscrapers grew from the city center, and then the skyline shrank from there as it spread out toward the edges.

With the sun setting on the other side, the light streaked across and kissed each building as the inhabitants turned their own lights on for the evening.

Truly, a metropolis.

As her MechWarriors entered the room and sat down at the table, she regarded every one of them with a stern look. She felt like that was how a captain of a soon-to-be-renowned mercenary unit would act.

Arkee and Evan arrived first, holding hands until they came to the threshold, but they parted once they stepped into the room. They were very professional about their public displays of affection. Never on the job, as it were. As always, they piloted their *Quickdraw* and *Locust*, respectively.

Dexter Nicks came next. He wasn't a particularly big or small guy. On a size chart, he'd fit neatly between Evan and Arkee. He had a bionic hand from an injury he didn't talk about and, despite his grim past, was easy enough to get along with, so long as nobody poked at old wounds. He piloted a 55-ton *Griffin* they'd found in a salvage yard and been able to repair with replacement parts they'd traded for. He was about as well equipped as Katie's *Kit Fox*, but had better heat dissipation and armor, meaning he could take a much heavier pounding.

The last MechWarrior to arrive was Rhiannon Ramirez. Of all the MechWarriors in Katie's command, Rhiannon was the one she'd most likely refer to as a loose cannon. She piloted the Fox Patrol's reclaimed *Marauder*, and was a holy terror in it. There was talk of Katie trading her *Kit Fox* for the *Marauder,* but there was something special about *Kagekitsune* she couldn't leave behind. There was some power and magic in her connection with the 'Mech. It was like destiny had guided her to it, abandoned after almost a century in the jungles of Jerangle. Nothing short of destiny.

The Fox Patrol was able to field a nice, round group for a pretty good attack group. A pair of heavy 'Mechs and a pair of lights, with one medium in between.

As long as they all worked together, there wasn't much that could stop them. That is, if they chose their jobs well and made sure they never walked into any situation outgunned.

Katie had done her best to learn those lessons as she'd managed the additional duties of commanding a merc unit.

It wasn't easy.

But she did her best.

Frankie came in last, grease stains on their clothes and face.

"Captain," Frankie said, leaning against the wall behind the conference table, "the hired hands have all been paid and are on their way. A few said they'd be willing to come back if we were jumping again any time soon."

"That's good to hear," Katie said. "And everything is tip-top with the DropShip?"

"As far as I can tell. While you all are doing your thing, I expect I'll be here working on diagnostics. We'll be ready to launch whenever you say the word."

"Excellent."

"So, what's the job, Cap'n?" Arkee said.

Katie grinned slyly. "I'm glad you asked that, Sergeant Colorado. The local magistrate of Vangelis City hired us because their petitions to the Prince of the Dominion and the Khan of Clan Ghost Bear have been refused. They were hesitant to hire mercenaries at first. Apparently there's a lot of baggage in their culture about hiring warriors, but I was able to convince them we could be very discreet and get out quickly."

Arkee's brow furrowed. "Are we going to be in trouble if the Ghost Bears find us here? They don't like mercs. At all."

"I mean, we'll be out before they know it. And according to the minister in charge of Vangelis City, there isn't any part of the Ghost Bear *touman* here on Kaesong. Did I pronounce that right? *Tao-man? Tow-man? Two-men?* Anyway, it doesn't matter. The point is, they need help, and it was faster for us to spend all that time jumping here than it was for them to keep trying to get help from the Dominion's government."

Arkee nodded at that, but she could tell he didn't like anything about the job.

"Don't worry," she continued, "this is going to be an easy job, and the minister offered to pay an inordinate amount of money for it. That's why we went with it."

"What's the job, then, Captain?" Ramirez asked.

"There's a minor bandit who's been terrorizing the people of Vangelis City. He's raised some infantry and ground vehicles, but the intelligence Vangelis officials sent over say they only have one 'Mech. So we'll be able to chew through them. We'll find their stronghold, root them out, and then it'll be game over. We take our money and get to go on our merry way."

"You have the next job lined up yet?" Nicks asked.

"Not yet. But it'll only be a matter of time."

"Are we going out with all five 'Mechs?" Evan asked.

"I think so, yes. No sense in letting them get the drop on us. What I thought was that you and I would take the recon positions. According to the minister, the target is hiding in a system of caves, through a wooded area and in a slot canyon. It's all south of the Vangelis, though these guerrilla attacks have happened against convoys in every direction around the city."

"Would it be smarter to set an ambush around a fake supply convoy?" Arkee asked.

"No. Apparently their tactics are to use minimal force when they're marauding. The only way to catch them all is to catch them in their base."

"Are we luring them out for a stand-up fight?" Nicks asked.

"Not necessarily. We're going to give them a fight where they are, even if we have to go into their caves, though I'd prefer if we didn't need to get that far."

Ramirez brushed a spot of lint off her uniform. "And they won't be expecting us?"

"That's the idea. They won't know we've been deployed. As far as the intelligence Vangelis has cobbled together, they won't have any idea we've arrived at all."

Nicks leaned back in his chair. "Who's to say that they didn't just watch our big, bloody DropShip land on the outskirts of town and are now counting down the minutes for our arrival?"

"According to the minister, there are DropShips arriving every few days anyway. The last one came in a couple of days ago. They hit it the day after, wagering that the DropShips were unloading goods they could steal."

"I dunno," Arkee said. "There's something about this I don't like."

Katie sighed. "Arkee, you've said that about every single mission we've been on in the last four years."

Arkee shrugged. "Fair enough, Cap'n."

"And let's be honest. It's five 'Mechs against one. I don't anticipate their infantry being that much of a problem. We can chew through them with ease."

Ramirez leaned forward, putting her elbows on the conference table, her hands balled into tense fists. "The only question I have is when do we move out?"

Katie glanced at the chronometer on her wrist. "First, I'll get you all the intel you need. Maps and topography. Frankie will load them into our 'Mechs. Then we'll leave in waves. The heavies will lead out. Then, Nicks, you'll go in your *Griffin*. Evan and I will take the rear, but since we move faster, we'll still arrive first and then scout the area. We'll begin the operation within the hour."

The all nodded and agreed with the general thrust of the plan.

With any luck they wouldn't have any problems at all.

OUTSKIRTS OF VANGELIS CITY
KAESONG
RASALHAGUE DOMINION
16 DECEMBER 3148

Katie's *Kit Fox* hummed to life as she settled into the command couch. Sometimes she worried that over the years it would get uncomfortable, or feel less and less like home. The opposite held true. Every time she sat down in the 'Mech, she felt more and more like it was the one place she truly belonged. Every scent, the oil and ozone, brought her to a different engagement she'd fought. But, through all of it, there was still the lingering scent of the Jerangle jungle. The heat of the fusion engine brought it up to the surface more than anything and reminded her of the place where she found her salvation.

The feel of the command couch beneath her, the springiness of the seat, made her feel as though she were wrapped up in a warm blanket. The same one her parents used to snuggle her in.

Back when they were alive.

Then, there were the little Scarecrow touches. The way the moving parts of the *Kit Fox* vibrated always took her back to times of working in his garage, dealing with the joint assemblies of various 'Mechs. Back in those days, they were all AgroMechs, but the *Kit Fox* still had a bit of that same feel.

It all made her feel like she was home.

"Heavies are on their way," Arkee reported.

"*Griffin* is go," Nicks said.

"You ready?" she asked Evan on his direct line.

"I'm always ready, Captain."

"All right," she said, waiting for their designated time to embark. "Let's do this."

Evan's *Locust* had to keep off its top speed so that Katie could keep up in her *Kit Fox.* They were still the two fastest 'Mechs in their lance though, and it wasn't long before they overtook the *Griffin*, and then the *Quickdraw* and the *Marauder.*

"Looking good, Foxes," Katie said as she passed the group.

And she meant it.

Now that they all had a similar color scheme, with the white fringes at the bottom, feathering up toward a rusty brown like a fox, they looked like a handsome fighting unit. And since she'd been able to bring them up to peak efficiency—with the help of Frankie, of course—the 'Mechs all purred like foxes, too.

It gave her a thrill to know that she wasn't just operating the 'Mech she piloted, but that she had four others to work with, each helmed by a competent MechWarrior who could execute her commands to the letter. It was an awesome display of power. She'd never felt more formidable in her life. And if they kept gaining reputation, they'd get registered with the

Mercenary Review and Bonding Commission and start climbing the ranks for real. Then maybe one day they'd be hired by one of the Great Houses. Or maybe they'd see combat as an elite unit in some important conflict, something that would turn the political balance for control of the Inner Sphere.

Maybe one day someone would sing songs of the Fox Patrol and tell stories of their exploits.

Katie beamed at the thought, her cheeks almost hurting from smiling so wide.

Looking at her viewscreen, Katie saw the other Foxes at the edges, where her rearview had been compressed into the 180 degrees of screen she had. In front of her were rocky crags and coniferous trees, with the road they were on leading right up to it. This was the path the raiders would take very time they came down to steal things from Vangelis. They likely had other ways out, though, probably lots of cave outlets and at least one or two back roads. It would have been a lot easier to ambush them if this was the only path in or out of their hole in the wall.

"You see anything, Evan?"

"Nothing yet, Captain."

As they headed deeper into the slot canyon, the sunlight faded further, cut off from the sky. The path up the center was wide enough for a 'Mech. A few snapped branches along the way showed them just where the enemy 'Mech had trampled through without a care, tearing branches as it moved. For the most part, though, the path was clear.

"Captain," Evan said, "Can I ask a question?"

"Shoot."

"Have you ever dealt with entrenched infantry?"

"No. Why?"

"Well, I'm just wondering how this plan is going to work."

"Me too." Katie looked down at her console readouts, wondering if there was anything to see. Nothing presented itself. She looked then to her viewscreen and toggled through displays, looking to see if there was anything that would tip off movement from the local guerrillas.

"I'm still not seeing anything," she told Evan.

"Same. I've got wide scans going on every instrument I can imagine, and I haven't seen anything. You know how far in they might be?"

"The topographical map says we're getting close."

"What are the chances that this is a trap?"

"You sound like your boyfriend."

"That's not an answer to my question."

"Why would it be a trap? We were hired by the local government to deal with these guys. Why would they trap us?"

"Take our 'Mechs."

"That's—I mean...possible? I guess?"

"I'd want our 'Mechs."

"I mean, yeah."

"Seriously though. This isn't ringing any alarm bells for you?" There was a strain of concern in Evan's voice she hadn't heard in a long time. And it seemed she only ever heard it when things were about to go south.

But it didn't seem apparent that anything *was* going to go south.

All they had to do was keep on steady, destroy the resistance, savage the lone bandit 'Mech, and eliminate the infantry. Easy as pie, right?

Katie got to thinking, then keyed Arkee onto the comm. "Arkee, why don't you watch our six? Face behind us, just in case they're trying to pull an ambush."

"You seeing anything suspicious?"

"No. Not yet. And that, in and of itself, is suspicious."

"Affirmative, Cap'n. I'll hang back and watch out for the eventual double-cross."

"Good." She switched her comm so the entire unit could hear. "Fox Patrol, keep your eyes open. We haven't spotted anything yet, but that's usually when trouble strikes. The *Quickdraw* is going to watch our six. The lights are going to continue reconnaissance and see what there is to see. Got it?"

"*Yes, sir,*" came the voices of Nicks and Ramirez. Arkee and Evan followed suit, not wanting to make it weird for the other two.

"The vanguard will fan out. The *Griffin* and *Marauder* will come up the center. Go now."

The slot canyon narrowed, but they spread out nonetheless as they got closer and closer to the end of the ridge. The element of surprise was likely gone since all five 'Mechs knocked over trees as they went. Even if a battle wasn't about to erupt, the serenity of this little piece of Kaesong countryside was going to be damaged for a generation.

The first explosion flared behind them.

So did the second.

The third, however appeared at the feet of Katie's *Kit Fox*, erupting in a great rent in the ground beneath them.

Land mines?

The damage indicators on her console flashed yellow at the legs.

"Everyone, full stop. Cease the advance."

"Mines?" Evan asked.

Katie wasn't sure. It could have been infantry. It could have been the raiders' 'Mech taking potshots for all she knew. But if Evan assumed it was mines too, that's likely what it was.

"Unknown. Run a scan."

"Affirmative, Cap."

While Evan went to work, Katie eyed everything around her, wondering what other surprises could await them. She cursed herself for even *being* surprised. Why would landmines be so out of the realm of possibility for her to envision?

She needed to get a lot better at her job if the Fox Patrol was going to become the renowned mercenary unit she knew they could be.

"Anyone else seeing damage?"

"No damage here, just a little shaken," Nicks said.

"Same," called out Ramirez.

"Nothing on my end," Arkee said.

"Good. Keep your eyes peeled though, eh?"

"Got it."

She switched her viewscreen to thermal imaging, hoping to pick out the heat of the bodies. If the infantry was around, would they be hiding in foxholes? Would they be up in the trees? Or would they be hidden in the caves?

In the distance, along the base of the trees on both sides of the road, tiny little red bodies were all lined up in a row. Were they dug into trenches?

She switched to a few different view modes, but couldn't see anything through the foliage. They were hidden pretty good.

"I've got infantry spotted on either side of the road. Sending the data now."

"Affirmative," Evan said. "I've got more mines up ahead. You can see the discolored dirt on the path. I'm marking them on your maps."

"Excellent. Weapons free then. Get in there and root them out."

"With pleasure," Evan said. But she somehow doubted he'd derive any pleasure from flushing out a bunch of infantry from their dug-in positions. He relished 'Mech combat. They were MechWarriors. They *all* preferred 'Mech combat. But Evan wasn't going to let the pursuit of enjoyment get in the way of doing the job.

His *Locust* took the lead position, its chicken legs stepping over the spots he'd tagged as mines. It wouldn't do well if he blew up before they'd even seen any real action.

Dancing through the minefield, the *Locust* looked like a drunk chicken without feathers, but he made it through safely.

"Careful," she said, as though he needed the reminder.

"I'm being careful."

She switched back to thermal and watched the little red bodies in the trenches get antsy as the 'Mech approached. They all gripped weapons of some type.

"What are they waiting for?"

Evan's response came not with his voice but with his machine guns. He let loose with a spray of bullets, peppering the entire area.

That had the infantry hopping mad, like little, red-hot hornets. They didn't pour out of their trench to launch their attack though, which is sort of what Katie had expected.

The last thing she expected was for them to detonate all the mines in the field at once.

Explosions filled Katie's view, and dirt flew high up in the air. She felt the concussive force of the detonations even through the sturdy frame of her 'Mech.

But she lost sight of the *Locust* through the blast, and the heat of the fire obscured all of the infantry she'd been keeping an eye on.

"Evan, what's the sitch?"

But Evan didn't respond.

This was a pattern with him. Arkee, too. They would get so focused on the smaller, albeit more dangerous, task at hand and forget to check in on the comm. On some level, she figured she should just admire their focus.

But she still needed the information.

"Evan, respond!"

Once the heat and the smoke cleared, she was surprised by what she saw.

The *Locust*'s legs were tangled up in a knot of heavy cable. Another booby trap. The mines were meant to separate the 'Mechs, then they launched a trap. The infantry valiantly tried to get close enough to Evan's stuck 'Mech to climb up the side, but the *rat-tat-tat* of machine-gun fire kept them back.

"I could use a little help here," Evan said finally.

Katie moved *Kagekitsune* forward, navigating over the pockmarks the mines had left on the trail. *How did they know we were coming?*

But maybe the raiders didn't know they were coming. Maybe they were just prepared for *any* incursion, and this was why the local authorities were powerless to do anything about it. Sure, these clowns only had one 'Mech, allegedly, but they were so well dug-in it looked like they could survive a prolonged siege.

When the Fox Patrol showed up, Katie was sure they had the raiders outgunned. But now that she saw how deep the infantry was really entrenched, she wondered if she'd actually brought enough firepower.

Maybe the Fox Patrol could use some infantry of their own, if they could afford it.

Mercenary work was expensive.

Katie fired through the trees with her lasers, hoping to clip some of the errant infantry. A closer look showed they were all clad in the same forest camouflage. A healthy mix of young and old. Every one of them was armed; some carried sidearms, other rifles.

Katie fired her lasers at the feet of Evan's *Locust,* obliterating a pair of soldiers gunning for him. Watching those people just evaporate didn't do much for her stomach. It was one thing to fire at a 'Mech and kill the pilot inside and not really have to think about it, but watching her lasers just incinerate actual, real-life human beings left her queasy.

"I think I've got a problem, Cap," Evan said.

She'd have time to mourn the dead later. "What's the problem?"

Evan didn't get a chance to answer. A flash of red light filled the area, and half the armor on Evan's right leg just seared off. The legs on the *Locust* were pretty thin as it was. He didn't have much armor to spare.

"Laser cannon, on a platform up ahead. They're hiding near the road."

"Take it out."

"Working on it."

The *Locust* struggled against the cables intertwined through its legs, designed to throw it off balance or trip it. Evan was too smart to get tripped up, but that didn't mean he still wasn't going to have a problem.

He didn't need to move to fire, though. All he needed to do was aim.

"Just shoot at it!" Katie said.

And he did.

A green flash burned her eyes, but she didn't see where it went. She couldn't see the gun platform anyway.

"Did you get it?" Katie said, pushing forward.

She fired her own lasers right at the infantry beyond the cables holding Evan in place. She winced as she boiled another member alive, but the shot had the desired effect of taking out the cables. She was grateful she couldn't hear the raider scream. "You should be free of the trap."

"Thanks for that." The *Locust* stepped forward, free of the entangling lines. The remaining infantry scrambled backward, no doubt falling back to the next defensible position.

He fired again, just as Katie got close enough to see the laser platform herself.

It wasn't anything fancy; just a hovertruck with a laser and an engine rigged in the back. Enough to power the laser and the truck and creep along at a slow pace. The truck fired again, but the shot flew wide, damaging only to the trees beyond them.

Katie found the forest beautiful, much different and more serene than the jungles she grew up near. She hoped they didn't set it ablaze: a forest fire wouldn't help any of them, though it would make a sensible tactic for the raiders' last stand.

"I'm here." Nicks had finally arrived with the *Griffin*. At 55 tons, it was almost twice the weight of Katie's *Kit Fox*, and she *felt* it coming. If she could, even through the dampeners and shocks in her 'Mech, she knew the bandits could, too.

There'd be no escape for them.

They had to know that.

Katie scanned the topographical data they'd been given, and found a clearing in front of the cave system. That's likely where the traps would be if they had another one to spring.

They'd likely expect the Fox Patrol to come at it head on.

"Nicks, push into the forest. I've marked a spot on your map as a waypoint. Approach that meadow in front of the cave system from the side. Evans and I will go from the front. Ramirez, you take the other flank. We'll catch them off-balance and in a crossfire. Arkee, keep on our six. We'll call if we need reinforcements."

"You folks get all the fun," Arkee said in mock disappointment.

"It pays to be the boss. On the other hand, if I die, you'll have to figure it out on your own."

"Don't talk like that, Cap'n. We'll get through this."

"We'll see."

"Evan, slow down. We'll give them time. We'll come to the clearing at the same time."

"Sure," he said, firing his lasers and machine guns at the ant-like infantry, scurrying away from him as they fell back.

She *had* to think of them like ants. She'd grapple with the rest later.

As Katie crept forward in her *Kit Fox,* she finally saw the next phase of the defenses: a wall in the road. There was a heavily guarded, fortified gate the laser truck could pass through. A shack for a guard stood next to it. A machine gun—which would be largely useless against 'Mechs—poked out of the front. Like the nest of a bird of prey. The wall itself was so flimsy that a 'Mech could kick through it or walk over it. No problem.

This must have been a layer of defense designed to keep the local militia out. And it would certainly have been effective against other infantry.

I wonder what we'll find in the clearing, she thought.

Because anything could be there.

So far, the intel had all been correct. Katie wondered how many locals had lost their lives to collect it. All of it seemed hard won, based on the fortifications.

Perhaps the locals were sneakier than they got credit for.

"Blast the guard shack," Katie told Evan, and he obliged.

Opening fire with his lasers, he melted the tin walls of the shack in a blink, along with whatever guards and infantry were inside.

Steam rose from the seared metal.

Katie opened fire on the gate with her lasers, and utterly obliterated the crossbar meant to keep vehicles out.

Nothing would stop the Fox Patrol.

More infantry scrambled away, doing their best to get clear of the incoming 'Mechs.

Katie smiled.

This was how things were supposed to go.

"Slow it down, Evan," Katie said. "Keep the pressure on, but we need to give the others time to get into position."

"Understood."

They both slowed down, taking careful steps.

"Doesn't look like there are any mines this far up," Evan said, evidently taking the time to sweep for them while they had a moment.

"I wouldn't imagine they would." Katie looked at the wall before them and suddenly wondered... "Wait."

"What?" Evan asked.

"I'm thinking we're still in for some more traps. First the mines, and now..." Instead of finishing her thought, Katie aimed her lasers at the wall on the side opposite the gate and let loose.

The large and small lasers lanced across the distance in a flash. The moment the beams hit the wall, a large explosion rocked the area. The shockwave knocked over the infantry already scrambling toward their next fallback position. Those too close to the blast charred black and dropped. Killed.

Katie wondered if whatever they were defending was worth their lives. But then she thought about the pay she'd be receiving for this particular mission and wondered whether her own life would be worth that. It probably wasn't, but at least she was *building* something.

"What the hell was that?" Evan asked.

"Just as I thought. They'd rigged the wall to blow and would've set it off as soon as we stepped over it. Target the other side and trigger any explosives they have over there."

Evan obliged, and this time, the explosion was even larger. It rent a deep gash in the ground. When the smoke cleared, the smoky field before them was littered in the bodies of the raiders. Those that could still stand ran even faster. Those that couldn't tried crawling out of the way, just in case they were in the path of a 'Mech that would stomp on them.

Katie made a conscious choice to ignore the horror and the blood.

"Keep it steady, Evan," she said.

Checking her topographical map and the transponders of the other 'Mechs, she saw they were all converging on the clearing in front of the cave.

"You all ready to step into this?" she asked.

"As I'll ever be," Evan said.

Nicks and Ramirez both responded with a much more professional "*Affirmative, Captain.*"

"Let's do it then. Watch out for more booby traps, but we go on my mark."

She knew that just up ahead, through that clearing, there would be something. And it could very well kill her. Or one of her Fox Patrol.

She knew their lives were on the line.

But all she felt was excitement.

The thrill of piloting a 'Mech.

She was a MechWarrior.

And this was what she was born for.

"Mark," she said coolly.

She pushed her *Kit Fox* forward in time with Evan's *Locust*, stepping over the remains of the wall and the craters in the ground from where they'd set off the explosions. The road bent around a slight and gentle curve, which they followed until they could see the cave ahead of them through the trees overhanging the road.

"There it is."

"We've got a problem here, sir," Ramirez said.

"What is it?"

"Unless my eyes deceive me and my console has been hijacked, that's a *Kodiak.*"

"Jesus Christ," Nicks said.

And as Katie and Evan crested the trees that blocked their view of the clearing, they saw it. It stood tall and proud in front of them, a massive, bulky BattleMech with humanoid legs and claws on each of its hands.

Katie gasped.

At 100 tons, the *Kodiak* nearly outclassed the entire Fox Patrol. The giant 'Mech was taller than everything at Katie's disposal, not to mention better equipped and much more heavily armored. The Ultra AC/20 autocannon jutting from its left torso could blow any single one of them to pieces in a single shot. Just the thought of it filled Katie with the distinct feeling she'd gotten into the wrong line of work.

The *Kodiak* stood even taller than the cave. It couldn't retreat inside. It had nowhere to go—its only recourse was to attack.

It was cornered.

According to her readouts, the *Kodiak* had enough speed and maneuverability to cover the distance between them in the time it would take them to open fire. The clearing didn't seem as small on the map as it did there with the *Kodiak* guarding its den.

The bandits must have salvaged it from a battle with Clan Ghost Bear. That would make the most sense.

But that didn't explain why Clan Ghost Bear didn't come back here, smack these fools around, and take back their 'Mech. That was fine with Katie that they didn't, though. She *wanted*

that *Kodiak* for the Fox Patrol. An assault 'Mech would put them over the top and in demand.

The only downside was finding ammunition. And even when it could be found, the price was exorbitant, if the owner was even willing to sell it.

As if to accentuate the point, the *Kodiak* let loose with a barrage of short-range missiles that spiraled toward Ramirez in the *Marauder.* It made sense for the pilot to pick the biggest target first. And to be honest, Katie was thankful they had. An equally valid strategy would've been to take out the smallest 'Mechs to begin with.

But there's as much wisdom in taking on the hardest target at the outset.

The missiles peppered the front of the *Marauder* as Ramirez moved into position, the explosions rippling across her legs, arms, and cockpit.

"Ramirez, you okay?"

"Nothing I can't handle."

True to her reputation, Ramirez held nothing back, firing her full complement of weapons at the *Kodiak* coming right for her. The crackle of bluish white from her PPC blasts, the flash of her medium lasers, and the explosive report of her autocannon lit up the meadow like a fireworks display.

The full alpha strike didn't even phase the damn thing.

"You've got to be bloody kidding me," Ramirez said, taking a step back in the *Marauder* and lining up another shot.

The bottom dropped out of Katie's hopes. Ramirez had unloaded on the *Kodiak*, and it didn't even look scratched. "Evan, hit that thing with everything you've got. Nicks, you too. Even your ammo suckers."

Katie had done everything she could to get the Fox Patrol to restrain from using their ammo-based weapons as often as possible rather than their lasers. Though the lasers were practically free, missiles needed to be replaced. But if there was a situation that called for all weapons on deck, it was a bloody Clan assault 'Mech.

"Arkee, we're going to need you," Katie called out. "Get up here."

"Negative, Captain," came Arkee's response.

Katie flushed red. "Are you disobeying a direct order?"

"Negative, Captain," Arkee said again. She heard a muffled explosion through the comm and a grunt from the MechWarrior. "There was another infantry ambush. More explosives. They've got me pinned."

Katie took a deep breath and wondered when a job would ever go according to plan. Maybe never? "Get up here as fast as you can. And don't die."

"On it, Cap'n," Arkee said through gritted teeth.

Katie couldn't help but stress about Arkee's fate in the background of everything else going on. Being the leader meant worrying about everything.

Evan would never forgive her if Arkee died, nor should he. But he wouldn't forgive her if she got the rest of them killed either, so she returned her attention to the *Kodiak.*

After angling into position by edging around the side of the clearing, Nicks fired a barrage of long-range missiles that streaked across the clearing, leaving a wake of smoke behind them. They scarred armor casings all across the back of the ursine 'Mech, but the *Kodiak* barely noticed the damage. It just kept closing in on Ramirez.

"Come on, you bastard," Ramirez said over the radio.

Katie ignored her and reminded everyone to keep closing in, flanking, and getting in shots on the *Kodiak.* "None of us are going to be able to take this thing solo. We've got to work together."

"We've got to work together faster," Ramirez said, her infamous nerves of steel shaking in her voice.

Katie and Evan unloaded with their lasers, doing their part to carve away enough armor so that they might be able to do some real damage to the goddamn thing.

"Let's get in closer," Katie told Evan. "Nicks, keep hammering it with your missiles."

"Got it, Captain."

Nicks, a consummate professional, unloaded with another volley. The projectiles crackled above the top of the *Kodiak,* with only a couple making impact, doing only the slightest damage. The pilot had still had their eyes on Ramirez's *Marauder.*

The *Kodiak* raised its hands, where all of its eight medium lasers were mounted, and stretched its claws out toward Ramirez.

"This guy just won't take a hint. I said I don't want to dance." Ramirez called out as though the *Kodiak* pilot could hear her. "I need some help!"

"Doing our best," Katie said, firing her own lasers at the charging bear of a 'Mech. She hit as much air as leg.

Evan did the same, but tagged an arm as well. They were going to need to do a lot better than that.

Why did it have to be an assault 'Mech?

The *Kodiak* let loose with its full spread of lasers. Beams lanced out and hit the *Marauder*'s arms and legs on either side. That was lucky for her on some level. She wasn't going to lose her cockpit immediately, but she was going to have a *lot* of damage and trouble navigating. Katie could see the melting at the joints and down the extremities.

"Ramirez, status."

"Not good. Red lights everywhere."

"Damn it. Everyone, hit 'em again."

Nicks opened fire with his last salvo of missiles, and they crashed into the *Kodiak* as it covered the last of the distance between it and the *Marauder.*

Not only did Ramirez fire her PPCs and her lasers, but her autocannon, too, but it just wasn't enough. Armor shattered and melted all over the massive 'Mech, but it still kept coming. *Did they reinforce the armor somehow?*

Again, the Fox Patrol just opened up with everything they could. There was no sense in holding back when a 'Mech that big and armored wraps its grizzly arms around you.

The *Kodiak* took the few hits that landed like some sort of prize fighter. The Foxes were going to need to figure out how to hunt bigger game like this without putting themselves into harm's way.

They had to put it down before it let loose with its AC/20, otherwise they would all be dead, one at a time, like it was nothing.

"What are they waiting for?" Katie asked to no one in particular.

Because if they lost Ramirez, she was going to have a full-on meltdown.

Katie pushed forward and fired her lasers once more. She wasn't going to be able to do it for much longer because the heat in her 'Mech rose with her temper. Sweat poured from her brow. She felt it practically pooling in her neurohelmet.

"I'm going in for a better shot," Evan said.

"Take it," Katie said.

The *Locust* bounded into the clearing, taking a strafing run at the *Kodiak* as it worked to push past and get out of Nicks' line of fire.

Evan's laser missed, and the *Kodiak* didn't even slow down.

We're never going to take it down if we don't hit it...

The *Kodiak* clawed at the *Marauder*, pulling armor from it in a vicious grappling attack.

Ramirez used her *Marauder*'s reinforced arms to batter the *Kodiak* back. "Eat this!" She knocked one of the enemy 'Mech's arms away and brought her *Marauder*'s arms smashing back into the center of the bear 'Mech, staggering it back a step. Then she fired again.

Katie couldn't see what damage it did, the *Kodiak*'s back was still turned to her, but Ramirez lit it up as though her lasers were a welding torch, sparks flying everywhere.

But something still struck Katie. "Why aren't they using the autocannon?"

"They want our 'Mechs!" Ramirez said. "It's the only explanation!"

The *Kodiak* pilot stepped forward again, encroaching further on Ramirez, tearing more armor off the *Marauder*.

Katie was scared to shoot for fear of hitting her already-compromised teammate. The last thing she wanted was to put Ramirez in an even worse situation. But what else could she do? The *Kodiak* was going to tear her apart otherwise.

It was a sound strategy for the *Kodiak* pilot, and Katie wondered if they were more experienced than she'd been led to believe. The locals made it sound as though the MechWarrior and the other raiders were just a bunch of scum. But everything else was adding up to make Katie believe that this pilot might be some renowned Clan warrior. Or former Clan warrior. *Could there be former Clan warriors?* She didn't even know.

The Clans were a giant mystery to her.

She'd heard stories.

She knew this *Kodiak* had originated with them, and anyone who would fight in a Clan 'Mech with this degree of ferocity was someone to be taken seriously. Clan 'Mechs *were* better in most ways than the Fox Patrol's 'Mechs. But could the *Kodiak* really stand up against four of them?

"Nicks, get in there and try to hit it with your PPC. Evan and I will keep pounding it with lasers. Stop missing, and let's melt its back open."

"Got it."

The *Locust* got out of the *Griffin*'s line of fire, and Nicks blasted the damn thing, singeing the *Kodiak* with a blue-white bolt from his PPC.

Katie hoped the back of the *Kodiak* wouldn't take much more, though she had no way of knowing. But she *knew* Ramirez couldn't take anything else.

She fired her lasers, but they flew wide. The *Kodiak* was in too close, fiercely tearing at her. Panicked in the frenzy, Ramirez could barely speak, let alone aim well enough to hit with any accuracy.

Katie edged forward and lined up a shot that wasn't going to hurt Ramirez, even inadvertently. She hit the firing stud for her lasers and watched the wash of green energy slag the last chunk of armor at the *Kodiak*'s back.

Finally, the damage exposed enough of the inner workings beneath the armor to feel like she was fighting an actual BattleMech instead of some invincible monster. "Good work, Foxes. I think we're finally cracking through."

"A little faster would be nice," Ramirez said through gritted teeth. She wasn't going to last much longer. Getting mauled by a *Kodiak* was not how Katie would ever recommend anyone spend their time. Ramirez did her best to dodge and deflect the *Kodiak*'s blows, like that boxer trapped in the corner, covering their body. Unfortunately, the *Marauder*'s guns weren't as helpful as those of a boxer.

Evan hit the *Kodiak* next with his laser.

It blew Katie's mind that the Clan 'Mech had more firepower than she and Evan together, but the two of them barely added up to half the *Kodiak*'s weight. And if she added up all the other things the *Kodiak* could do, it probably outclassed any *three* of the 'Mechs in their unit. But there was no way it could take out the four of them.

Right?

"I'm out," Ramirez said.

What she meant didn't become immediately apparent until the *Kodiak* let go of the *Marauder*. It didn't so much as let go as *shove* the 'Mech down. The *Marauder* fell like a cut tree, crashing to the ground. Then Ramirez's 'Mech vanished from Katie's display, completely offline.

That's gonna leave a mark.

The *Kodiak* turned toward the rest of them, and that really just pissed Katie off. All that work exposing its back was all for nothing, unless they could get behind it again. But that seemed less and less likely because it was already at the edge of the clearing, with its back to the dense trees and fallen *Marauder*.

The *Kodiak* backed up, deeper into the trees, making a rear approach impossible without getting blown to smithereens on the way. They were going to have to start all over again with its front, which was better armored than its back. The *Kodiak* took aim at Evan's *Locust* first, its closest target, unleashing the full force of its lasers against him.

Fortunately, Evan was moving fast enough that half of the shots missed, but that didn't stop half the armor of the *Locust*'s head from turning into melted slag. Molten metal splashed to the ground and hardened almost instantly.

Katie took in a deep breath and almost suffocated on it in the heat of her cockpit.

As she strafed to the side and fired her lasers at the *Kodiak* again, the warning lights for her temp gauge screamed at her.

This must be what hell feels like.

Katie didn't know what else she could do. They'd expended most of their ammo-based weapons, and were heating up at an alarming rate.

They were also down one 'Mech.

The *Kodiak* had made the right call in going for the *Marauder* first and then turning on the rest of them.

"Evan, status."

"I've had better days."

"I bet. Let's do a hit-and-fade. We're both more maneuverable, so let's just try to keep it confused. We'll stay fast and light, and hit it with everything we've got until we don't have anymore. Get around it, see if you can get it to show us its back. Nicks and I will blast it."

"Affirmative, Cap," Evan said.

"Got it, Captain," came Nicks.

Nicks fired his PPC at the *Kodiak*. It was a good hit, ablating chunks of armor from the front of the 'Mech, but it wasn't enough to break it open. Katie fired again, but with her coming around and getting into position, she couldn't get a solid hit.

For his part, Evan kept trying to get behind the *Kodiak*, laying down suppressing fire the whole time. Katie hoped it would work. As the *Locust* got closer, surely the *Kodiak* would switch targets and expose its back to the other Foxes. Right?

As Evan got closer, it became painfully apparent that the *Kodiak* wasn't taking the bait.

Katie growled in frustration as the *Kodiak* just cycled targets and launched a salvo of SRMs at Nicks' *Griffin,* staggering it backward. The missiles burst all across his front, and all Katie could think of was how much this mission was going to cost them. She just hoped it wouldn't cost them any lives either.

I can't handle anyone dying on my orders. But if I'm not prepared for that, then maybe I'm in the wrong business.

Sweat poured from her face and arms as she forced her 'Mech forward, getting closer to the *Kodiak* for her attack run. Her cooling vest had its work cut out for it. She only had enough missiles for one salvo. She'd been saving them for a tight spot, and she couldn't figure a spot tighter than this.

Her computer locked on, and she pulled the trigger. The SRMs corkscrewed from the *Kit Fox* and drilled into the *Kodiak* in a brilliant cascade of fire.

But still it stood.

Fat lot of good that did.

The *Kodiak* looked no worse for wear, save the pockmarks where the missiles hit. That 'Mech's durability was *almost* enough to make Katie want to trade up from *Kagekitsune,* but her 'Mech was a good luck charm. She couldn't see herself giving it up willingly.

It had been her life.

Nicks' *Griffin* moved forward and fired its PPC at the *Kodiak*—a glancing blow. Sure, it ablated a chunk of armor, but it just didn't seem like they could do enough damage to it.

The *Kodiak* returned fire with another salvo of missiles; they roared across the clearing and smashed into the *Griffin.* It swayed back, as though Nicks struggled to keep the 'Mech upright.

"Evan, will you get behind it already?" Katie called out. If the *Kodiak* wasn't taking the bait from the *Locust,* she'd move in on the other side too. If they could force it to pick a target and expose its back to one of them, they would be able to put it down.

Otherwise, there was every chance it would put them down instead. Every 'Mech they lost reduced their chances of beating it. If they lost Nicks and the *Griffin,* what chance did two light 'Mechs have against this monstrous beast?

Katie tacked the *Kit Fox* to her right and watched ahead of her as Evan's *Locust* tacked to his left but matched her movements.

The *Kodiak* wouldn't bother with them, though. It just kept backing up, protecting its damaged rear armor and keeping laser-like focus on the *Griffin.*

They're going to take us all down! Panic and the intense heat gripped Katie as she opened fire with her lasers one more time. She wanted this to work. She *needed* it to work.

This one 'Mech couldn't be the end of the Fox Patrol.

Nicks fired his PPC, and a burst of blue light flayed the armor from the *Kodiak*'s right arm. Evan fired his lasers too.

"It's been a pleasure," Nicks said, surveying the inevitable.

The *Kodiak* reached out, aiming its laser-battery claws right at Nicks.

Time slowed for Katie.

She wanted to scream.

She wanted to do *something.*

If she could have leaped across the distance and put herself between the *Kodiak* and the *Griffin,* she would have.

But she didn't have to.

Explosions staggered the back of the *Kodiak,* pushing it forward, robbing it of the chance to fire on the *Griffin.*

"What the—?"

It hung there in the air for a moment before crashing forward.

In the space where it had been stood Arkee in his trusty *Quickdraw.*

"Sorry about the lack of communication, Captain," he said. "Those explosions knocked out a lot of my electrical systems, and I couldn't get them back online. But I'm here now, and everything's working."

"Arkee, I could kiss you right now," Katie said.

"Hey," came Evan's voice, predictably.

"You did the right thing."

"Well, between the data you all were sending and the radio chatter, I figured this approach would be the best way to help."

"You were absolutely right. Now let's mop up the rest of the caves, collect our pay, and take the *Fox Den* far away from this place."

"What do you mean you can't pay?" Katie verged on screaming into the radio from her office beside the bridge of the *Fox Den.*

"The minister deeply apologizes for the ruse," the administrative assistant said. "But we needed to deal with the bandits, and simply don't have the resources to pay you."

The minister didn't even have the guts to tell me himself.

"We have a contract!"

"If you'll notice in the fine print, there was a clause allowing us to renege under certain financial conditions, conditions which, unfortunately, have been met."

"What are we supposed to do?" she asked.

But there was no answer on the other end. There was nothing that could be done.

Katie would, naturally, report this, to any person or institution who would listen. She'd scream about this story in every bar and merc hangout on Galatea...if she ever made it there.

She sighed heavily.

She didn't want to tell the group any more than the local minister wanted to tell her.

She'd already assembled the briefing for the after-action report, so the other Foxes were waiting in the conference room already. They wanted to know more about the *Kodiak* and the pilot, but the pilot had vanished by the time the cleanup operation had ended and they'd gotten around to investigating the assault 'Mech. The first thing they discovered was why the *Kodiak* never fired its autocannon. It wasn't because the bandits wanted to take their 'Mechs, but because they didn't have any ammo for it.

Also, from what Katie could piece together, the leader of the bandits *had* been a Ghost Bear, but she'd flunked out of being one, or something. Katie didn't quite understand the Clans.

But that wouldn't be the big news they needed to hear. She had to stroll in there and tell them all the terrible news, too.

They'd be stuck here on Kaesong for a while.

Maybe she could at least negotiate room and board.

Thankfully, she'd put full salvage rights in the contract. That frustrated her. She'd have to sell the scraps of the *Kodiak* to keep everyone fed and get to the next job instead of keeping it to tinker with.

"Damn it!" she said to herself.

The door for the conference room opened, and she stepped inside, smiling wide.

"Well, friends, I have good news and bad news..."

Ah, the life of a mercenary captain...

GRIFFIN
MEDIUM–55 TONS

ACS

KODIAK
ASSAULT–100 TONS

MARAUDER
HEAVY—75 TONS

FOUR
A FOX ON GALATEA

CONFEDERATE-CLASS DROPSHIP *FOX DEN*
GALATEA
20 FEBRUARY 3149

"Ever since I was a little girl, I dreamed of going to Galatea one day," said Captain Katie Ferraro, the young commander of the Fox Patrol, as she stared longingly out the DropShip window at the swirled marble of a planet below.

"It's not so great," Dexter Nicks, one of the MechWarriors in her command, said from across the room. Only the pair of them were on the observation deck for the landing. The rest were off somewhere—buckled in, presumably—ready to make it to Galatea.

"What makes you say that?" She turned to look at him for just a moment, not wanting to tear her eyes from the heavenly sight before her.

He pointed his bionic finger out the window and scratched the graying scruff on his chin with his other hand. "I mean, it's just a place like any other."

"Easy for you to say. You've been lots of places."

"Wish I hadn't been to most of them."

"Well, how can I know I don't want to go to a place if I don't ever go there?"

"How can you tell you don't want to eat food if you haven't eaten it before? Sometimes it just looks or smells funny. Galatea looks and smells funny. Like mercenary sweat and battered 'Mechs everywhere. The whole place reeks of oil. And desperation from every merc unit in the Inner Sphere trying to make a name for themselves. They'll eat you alive down there if you're not careful."

Katie's grin couldn't be contained. "It sounds perfect."

"Heh," Nicks snickered. "For you, I bet it would be."

"You've been here before?"

"Yeah, a few times. When I signed up with other units. Fought here and there. Fought in one of the cages down a time or two, and I wouldn't recommend it."

"I envy the life you've led sometimes," Katie said, panning her eyes back and forth against the vision of Galatea in the window. There were spots across its globe that swirled in blue and patches of deep green where forests clustered around rivers and oases, though much of the world had browned out with the heat. But there was nothing about the planet below that Katie didn't find beautiful.

Just like she'd imagined it in her dreams.

"I wouldn't envy too much," Dexter said. "Both paths we took led us to the same place. This rusty tin can hurtling through space, right to Galatea this fine January day."

"I mean, I get that, but your path to get here was a lot more interesting."

His bionic arm whirred as he flexed it. "Sure," he said. "More interesting."

"You've seen so many things and piloted so many 'Mechs and fought against so many foes and lived to tell the tales."

Nicks shrugged. "Barely."

"And now you're here. In my command. Part of the scrappiest mercenary unit this side of Terra."

Nicks barely contained a sigh. The age difference between him and his captain showed through like starlight on a cloudless night. "Is that what we're calling ourselves now? 'Scrappy'?"

"You have a better word for it?"

"No, I suppose I don't."

"Then you get to live with 'scrappy.'"

The grizzled veteran more than a decade her senior shook his head as the DropShip's engines throttled up a bit, fine-tuning the final braking maneuver to Galatea.

"Scarecrow used to tell me stories about Galatea, but I'll be honest, I don't think he'd ever been."

"Scarecrow?"

"The man who raised me after my parents died. 'Mech tech. Best I've ever seen. He taught me everything I know about fixing 'Mechs and captaining a merc crew. I feel like I've mentioned him before... Anyway, he told me there were so many wars fought here. And it changed hands so many times, but it always stood. This was the one place a mercenary could make an honest living."

"The one place they can make a *dishonest* living, too. And really, we've been making an honest living everywhere you've taken us, and you've never even been to Galatea."

Katie didn't acknowledge him. "There's something magical about this place. Where everyone comes together to find exactly the right crew they need for the job. When I asked about the Kell Hounds, owing to that's where my *Kit Fox* came from, Scarecrow told me once about Morgan and Patrick Kell putting down a religious insurrection on the planet by the skin of their teeth. They fought off cultists led by a man named Poore, and when a MechWarrior is about to get outmaneuvered by a smarter adversary like Poore did, they say you've been dealt a 'Poore man's hand.'"

"I don't think anyone says that."

Katie made no indication she had heard him. She just stared wistfully out the viewport at the oncoming planet. "I really can't wait to see it."

"You'll see lots of illicit 'Mech fighting, too," Nicks said with derision.

Katie turned to him, smile beaming across her face. "Oh, I plan on it."

"Just, be careful out there, Captain."

"I'm always careful."

Nicks simply nodded his head. "Uh-huh."

Katie's attention turned back out to the window. "I can't believe the *Fox Den* is going to be at Galaport."

"Well, that's where you land ships on Galatea, so it makes all the sense in the world to me."

"Galaport," Katie practically whispered again in awe, wonder never leaving her face. "It's going to be the best time I've ever had."

To that, Katie was glad Dexter Nicks kept his mouth shut.

GALAPORT
GALATEA
21 FEBRUARY 3149

Katie couldn't contain her excitement while waiting for Frankie Fischer, the Fox Patrol's lead 'Mech tech and engineer, to open the *Fox Den*'s doors. She wanted to set foot on Galatea more than anything, and she didn't want to wait a single minute more. She'd been dreaming of this day for as long as she knew there was a place called Galatea, where mercenaries went to live and work. Ever since the treaty with ComStar long, long ago made Galatea a hub for mercenaries across the Sphere. That's where all the greats went.

No one else aboard seemed to understand or share her excitement. Evan and Arkee were, besides her, the first two Fox Patrol members. They were terrible with the business aspect of merc work, even if they were terrific 'Mech jocks. They should have been beyond excited to see Galatea. And Nicks, he'd already been there; he should have been twice as excited because he knew how great it was. The last of her MechWarriors, Rhiannon Ramirez, was probably more interested in avoiding Nicks than she was in playing tourist, ever since they'd broken up.

Neither of them really talked about it. And Katie had been playing mediator between them ever since. It was obnoxious, but she was the captain, so it was her job to keep the unit together.

If they weren't going to make the most of their time on Galatea, though, that was their own problem, because she was going to make the most of hers. To hell with them if they didn't see the opportunity and wonder before them. And she would get them a great gig out of it. No question.

Katie's heart leaped as the door squeaked, ready to open. It started to descend, and the blast pit they'd landed in would be connected right to the hub of Galaport, and she couldn't handle the excitement. Her leg bounced, and butterflies fluttered violently around in her stomach.

Katie figured this might have been what it felt like when people talked about love, but she'd never experienced it for another person before. Just 'Mechs. And merc work. And the glory of well-oiled machines everywhere. Paradise, really.

The door descended and opened out onto a ferrocrete pad cut into one side of the blast pit. Beyond the threshold was the solid ground of Galatea and her first step would bring her to a place where so many legends had trod—through the storied history of the devastating Succession Wars all the way to the Blackout, which was still making communication across the Sphere long and difficult. Most recently, as far as Katie had heard, there had been conflict with Clan Jade Falcon on Galatea. The Galatean League stood defiant, having driven away the Falcons just four short years prior, leaving the planet once more a beacon for the best mercenaries in the galaxy.

At least that's what Katie told herself.

She couldn't help but smile.

Just as she went to take her first step, the voice of Arkee Colorado stopped her. "Hey, Cap'n, do you have a second?"

Arkee had a knack for interrupting everything Katie wanted most in the world at the worst possible second.

Katie took her step, then pivoted, annoyed. "Arkee. Yes. Of course. What do you want, *right now*. At this very second. Just as I'm about to set foot on a world brimming with the history of legendary MechWarriors..."

Arkee, a big man with black skin and a blacker beard, stood before her, narrowing his eyes in concern. "You okay, Cap'n?"

"I'm fine. What do you need?"

"Because if this is a bad time, I can wait." He raised his hands in surrender. He knew he'd upset *something*. "I mean, I don't want to stop you."

He extended his arm toward the boarding ramp like a maître d' welcoming her to a fancy restaurant.

"No, it's fine," Katie said. "I'd rather deal with it now than later. What do you need?"

"Well, there's a little thing I wanted to talk to you about..."

"So you said. If it's little, can it wait?"

"Well, Evan and I were...well, we were thinking about getting married tomorrow. And we wanted you to be there."

"Thinking about *what*?" Katie wasn't sure she heard him right.

"Getting married."

"I thought you two *were* married. You already call him your husband."

Arkee shifted from foot to foot and he kept rubbing his hands together. Sweat beaded on his brow. "I mean, I do. But, you know, that was just a commitment ceremony. We were really hoping to get married somewhere special."

"Oh." Katie didn't know what to say. The annoyance she felt melted away into feeling touched. "And you two want me there?"

"We wouldn't have it any other way."

"I underestimated you two. I thought you didn't care about Galatea at all. Where are you getting married?"

"We're hoping for the Archangel."

When he said that, a tingle ran up Katie's spine. "*The* Archangel? The Cathedral of St. Michael, patron saint of MechWarriors?"

Arkee nodded.

Katies knees got wobbly.

"That was definitely on my list of places to visit, Arkee. I'd love to be there. Tell Evan I wouldn't miss it for the world. When tomorrow?"

"We don't know yet. I'll let you know. We still have to arrange it with the priest, if we can. If not, it'll be somewhere. Or maybe we'll wait until we make planetfall somewhere even more special."

"More special than *Galatea*? How dare you? You're MechWarriors, Arkee. Act like it."

Arkee smiled. "So you'll come?"

"Of course I'll come. And we'll stay planetside as long as it takes for you to get a quick ceremony at the Archangel. That would be *amazing*. Do you need anything from me?"

"No. Just to come. I'll let you know a time for certain."

"Oh, Arkee, I'm so happy for you both!"

"I thought you might be. Just wanted to catch you before you left. I know you're excited to get on the surface."

"I mean, I am, but I've also got my first meeting with a prospective job broker tonight, so I'm just eager to get us some work."

That wasn't a lie. During the voyage to Galatea, Katie had spent most of that time following up on contacts to try getting the Fox Patrol some work, and a meeting had been arranged already. Arkee and Evan could afford to go sightseeing, but none of them would eat if she didn't get them a contract.

"I'm sure you won't lead us wrong, Cap'n. You haven't yet."

"That's not what you said after Kaesong."

"Kaesong wasn't your fault."

"That wasn't what you said after the Jocularity Situation."

"That one *was* your fault."

"See?"

"You're doing the best you can."

"Yeah." She nodded and smiled. She *was* doing the best she could. "Now, if you'll excuse me."

Arkee straightened up into a stiff salute, as though saluting was something they did in the Fox Patrol. She offered him a half-hearted return salute, and he marched right back into the innards of the DropShip.

Katie turned back toward the egress, ready to set foot on Galatea for the first time.

And then someone cleared their throat.

"Excuse me, Captain," came a voice. Ramirez.

Katie closed her eyes and suppressed a groan before spinning back around to find out what the hell *she* needed that was so urgent. "Yes?"

"Oh, everything okay?" Rhiannon asked when she saw Katie's face. Katie knew it was tight and stiff. She tried with every facial muscle to not look annoyed and frustrated, but that probably only made her look more so.

"Fine. Just fine. What do you need, Ramirez?"

Ramirez and Katie both had raven-black hair, but that was where their resemblances ended. Where Katie always seemed to have her hair pulled up into a sloppy bun, Ramirez's hair looked as though she had stepped out of an advertisement for hair-care products. Where Katie seemed to perpetually have a grease or oil stain *somewhere* on her face, Ramirez always looked flawless. Where Katie sort of melted into her baggy jumpsuit—always in the standard rust red of the Fox Patrol—Ramirez wore a black uniform with a Fox Patrol patch and red accents that snugged right against her. She was taller than Katie, and thicker, too. And with a much darker complexion.

They were like opposites, really.

Ramirez took her hands from her hips and folded them across her chest. "Can I come with you? Out to Galatea City?"

"I mean, I'm going to wander and then meet with a job broker. If you want to come along, I have no objections. Why?"

"Dexter. Says he's staying aboard, and the last thing I want is to be alone with him on this ship. Not after how things went."

"Oh. I mean… You know Frankie will still be here, I think. And their tech crew." Katie's annoyance faded as soon as she remembered she'd be going to Galatea.

"I don't really… Uh…" Ramirez really kept to herself on the ship and seemed to avoid Frankie and the techs. It couldn't have been their personality, because Katie fit right in with the 'Mech techs, and Ramirez got along well enough with her. Or maybe she only got along with her because she was the captain?

Katie didn't know for sure, but maybe this little field trip would be enough to find out. "Right. Got it. You can come with. I don't mind at all. But we're going, like, *right now.*"

"Understood, Captain."

Katie eyed the pistol strapped in a leather holster on Ramirez's hip. "Expecting trouble?"

"Always," she said without a hint of a smile.

"Let's get to it, then."

Katie turned around and marched. It didn't matter what anyone else needed. She was setting foot right that minute if she had to kill someone to do it.

GALATEA CITY
GALATEA

Katie couldn't believe how big Galatea City was. And how far from Galaport it seemed. She and Ramirez took a light-rail train that connected the spaceport to the city proper, and through the train car's reinforced-glass window she caught her first sight of the city from the ground.

It didn't matter that Galatea City looked like an industrial wasteland on the edges with ivory towers made of glass at the central hub of the city. It took Katie's breath away.

It was everything she wanted to see in a city where so much history had happened. She thought about what it must have looked like in the late 2700s, before ComStar made it the hub it was now. How small would the city have looked back then, as it stood on the precipice of becoming *the* place for mercenaries? Scarecrow had always spoken with so much fondness for that golden era of MechWarriors and thought the entire Inner Sphere had gone to hell as soon as the Clans arrived on the scene, but Katie didn't hold to those ideas. There were so many things for her to love about the time they were in right then. For one, she had her pick of 'Mechs throughout history, if she could get her hands on them. And the Clan technology that had been infused in Inner Sphere 'Mechs or had spurred the innovation to make them better had improved everything about being a MechWarrior. Perhaps it was nostalgia for the Great Houses? They were still around, though. They just had to compete with the Clans now.

But for a mercenary, that just meant so many more potential clients.

She and Ramirez passed through the industrial parts of town that housed the arenas where MechWarriors and mercenaries jockeyed for the favor of job brokers or fought for entertainment and gambling as well. Then they strolled through the shops and warehouses where the damaged or destroyed 'Mechs from the fights would be salvaged and repaired to fight another day. There was something magical about all of it to Katie.

She'd never seen a place so dedicated to the life she wanted to lead, and she realized she could die happy on Galatea knowing she was, for the first time, in a place where everyone, for the most part, loved piloting 'Mechs as much as she did.

Glorious.

The train pulled into the station in the heart of Galatea City's downtown, and the view had shifted considerably from Galaport to here. The buildings practically touched the clouds at the top of the sky and didn't stop. Nicks was right about the smell, too. Katie breathed it in like a favorite meal. Oil and ozone alongside the stink of garbage and sewage that permeated the back of any big city. But then on top of that were the food vendors, battling back against the bad odors, cooking up street-food delicacies from a hundred different worlds, and even Terra itself.

Hovercars and hovertrucks and all manner of wheeled vehicles kept the city bustling, but there were countless pedestrians. The narrow streets were much better for walking than taking cars, and Katie preferred it anyway.

"Wow," she said. Maybe to Ramirez, but maybe just to herself. Even she didn't know. "Have you ever seen a city so beautiful?"

Ramirez looked around and shrugged. "I'm sure there's a better part of town."

"Maybe. But I wanted to stop here and walk. I wanted to get the full effect."

"Right, then. Guess I knew what I was in for when I asked to come."

"You sure you asked just because of Nicks?"

"Yes."

"Because this, to me—" Katie gestured to the city in front of them, "—this is all beyond belief."

"That's why I like you, Captain."

"You know, when we're not on duty, 'Katie' is fine. I always feel weird being called 'Captain.'"

"Anything you say, Katie."

Katie didn't even realize she'd started walking down the street. Using the noteputer she'd brought along, she pulled up a map of the area and took them down a few streets, where they turned a corner to a much older part of town. The buildings were shorter, and there, at the end of the street, was the thing she was looking for.

"Isn't it *breathtaking*?" she asked Ramirez, but the question may well have been rhetorical.

"What am I looking at?"

"The Archangel," Katie said with awe.

At the end of the street stood the Cathedral of St. Michael, just as it had stood for the last 600 years. The building itself looked like something terrifically Gothic, plucked from the ancient history of Terra—stone and flying buttresses, bell towers that reached to the sky. The stained-glass rose window at the front of the cathedral, just above the door, featured a MechWarrior with the wings of St. Michael, standing in front of a *Locust*. Perhaps the MechWarrior was meant to be St. Michael himself.

He'd been the patron saint of warriors from time immemorial, but the MechWarriors adopted him not long after the advent of the first BattleMechs. And when mercenaries of all denominations had descended on Galatea, the old Catholic Church, even before the split with the New Avalon branch, thought Galatea was a place that needed a bishop and a cathedral.

The gables all housed statues of famous MechWarriors and martyrs from history.

"Oh," Ramirez said. "The church."

"That's not just any church. It's the Cathedral of St. Michael, patron saint of MechWarriors."

"Cool."

"Are you going to the wedding tomorrow?"

"Wedding?"

"Oh. Arkee and Evan said they were getting married tomorrow, if they could. And they were trying to make it at the Archangel. Maybe I shouldn't have said anything."

"No, it's fine. I just thought they were already married."

"Me too. But those two speak a language all their own."

"True enough."

"The cathedral's beautiful though, isn't it?"

"Sure."

"That stained glass is original, you know."

Ramirez's brow scrunched up, surely wondering about how that could be possible.

"Whenever war came here, the bishops and locals would take the stained glass out of the building and hide it, packed in crates. They've reinforced it some over the years, too, I'm sure. But with how much fighting Galatea has seen, we're lucky to see it still. Hell, that the stained glass has lasted for that long at all is some sort of miracle. If there really is a St. Michael, if you believe in that sort of thing, he must really be looking out for that church."

Ramirez looked at the cathedral and then back and forth up the street. Unimpressed. "Where you meeting the job broker?"

Katie heaved out a breath. "At a club called the Broken Locust. It's in the area. They seem to like *Locust*s around here."

"So why'd you come this way?"

"Well, I'd picked the spot because I wanted to see the cathedral first. And I gave myself enough time to go in and check it out, but if that's where Arkee and Evan are getting married, I'm sure I'll see the inside soon enough. So we can just do some sightseeing until we have to be at the club."

"I bet the club is really interesting."

"I mean, it's a club. I checked into the history. It's had a bunch of different names over the years. Nothing significant has happened there."

"I bet they have something to drink."

"Oh, it's definitely a club, so I'm sure they do. But I'm going to see what else there is around here we could see instead of the inside of the Archangel."

"I mean, I'm sort of thirsty."

"I see. Well, I guess we can go straight to the Broken Locust if you want."

"That sounds great."

Katie tilted her head and squinched her eyes, thinking about the view of the map she'd studied, trying to remember which direction the Broken Locust would be. When she figured out it was straight ahead, then right, then left, then left again, situated a block down—roughly behind the Archangel, as the crow flew—she started walking, and Ramirez followed dutifully behind her. None of the history had her interested, but when there was alcohol on the line, she sure as hell kept up.

Katie couldn't *force* her MechWarriors to care about things as utterly fascinating as Galatea's past or the weight of history she felt when looking at the Archangel, but she could still be miffed about it. As they walked, she kept her eyes on the church for as long as she could before they had to take that first right turn. Even then, when she had her back to the church, she spun around every few steps, almost making sure the church was still there, still real. Because even now she couldn't believe she was on Galatea. Parked at Galaport. Walking through Galatea City.

Seventeen-year-old Katie Ferraro would have died.

The Broken Locust was like other clubs across the Inner Sphere, only more so. It got its name from the shattered *Locust* cockpit hanging above the bar in the center of the room. The outer walls were covered in murals of famous 'Mech battles from over the centuries, mainly ones involving what looked like the Gray Death Legion.

Katie always thought that was a silly name for a 'merc unit. She understood the commander had named it after himself, and Grayson "Death" Carlyle was a storied commander, no question. Katie had read stories about him taking down 'Mechs with very little but his wits and bare hands, and knew he'd been a legend. But the unit's name still sounded like it was invented by someone trying a little too hard to sound cool. Katie decided she wouldn't say that part out loud, especially not to anyone in a bar so devoted to the Gray Death Legion. Even if the folks at the Broken Locust did misspell it "Grey Death Legion" on half of the murals, with no consistency whatsoever.

The din in the saloon never rose above a dull roar, and the music that covered over it was nothing more than the tickling, sedate piano tunes that had been in fashion decades prior.

Ramirez seemed rather dejected by that. "You said 'club,' I figured there would be dancing."

"No," Katie said, close to Ramirez, not wanting to broadcast too loudly for fear of anyone overhearing her. "I was told this was the sort of place you could have a meeting. Loud enough for your voice to not carry, not so loud that you have to shout to be heard."

"Great," Ramirez said, rolling her eyes.

Katie pretended not to notice. And maybe she'd fooled Ramirez into thinking that she hadn't, but Katie saw it. She knew what Ramirez thought. It made sense, too, given Ramirez's personality. She wanted a party. She referred to so many of their 'Mech engagements as 'parties,' too.

"So," Ramirez said, "who are we meeting?"

"I think that's him, right there," Katie said. She pointed to a darkened corner at the back of the room. A booth where a man sat in the dark, right below a part of the mural where a *Marauder* had been destroyed at the hands of a *Locust*. Well, not really their *hands*, Katie thought. *Locust*s didn't have hands.

The man's dark complexion practically blended him into the shadow. He chomped on an unlit cigar and sipped from a whiskey tumbler.

"Who is he?"

"Didn't get a name. I was told this was where to meet him, though. It was a contact of a contact we ran into two or three jobs back."

"The Lichtenstein Situation?"

"Yeah. McPherson. She mentioned she'd used this guy as a broker. He didn't like names, so we wouldn't have to give one either. And this is his usual spot."

"That was a long time ago. And she must have dealt with him even further ago than that. You sure this is who we're going to meet?"

"Yeah. I made contact through a middleman while we were on our descent. I told them who recommended us, and wired their finder's fee over, and they gave me directions here."

Ramirez shrugged. "Okay. You're the captain."

Katie stepped down the stairs into the main part of the Broken Locust and headed straight for the bar. "We'll get a drink first," she said, as though Ramirez needed an explanation for why someone would go into a bar and order a drink.

More than anything, she just needed some sort of liquid courage. She hadn't been much of a drinker in the past, she was too young to do much, but Arkee and Evan had taken her out drinking a few times after jobs, and it had caused a bit of a thirst in her. Never to excess, though. She didn't touch the stuff before jobs or really on the DropShip at all. But Arkee and Evan drank a lot. And so did the tech crew. And Ramirez. Also Nicks. Frankie, too. In fact, it seemed Katie was the only member of the Fox Patrol who didn't drink to excess at times. She wouldn't feel bad about having one drink at the Broken Locust.

As she got to the bar, she realized this *would* be drinking on the job, in a technical sense.

Damn it.

The bartender, a woman with a gray updo, a red dress, and a matching scarf tied around her neck, approached Katie. "What'll it be?"

"I'll, uh, take an UrbanMech."

"Sure thing." The bartender pulled the peach schnapps and orange juice and mixed it in equal parts for Katie before looking over to Ramirez. "You?"

"Whiskey, please. Neat."

"Well or top shelf?"

"What's your top shelf?"

"We've got a twelve-year McCracken and an eighteen-year Sugar House."

"Sounds good but pricey. I'll take the well."

"You got it."

After the bartender slid Katie's fuzzy UrbanMech across the bar, she pulled up a damp shot glass from under the counter, turned it right side up, and filled it with cheap whiskey from the spigot.

Katie turned, smiled at Ramirez, and gestured with her glass to indicate she wished to clink them together. "To a new job in the big leagues..."

"To the big leagues," Ramirez parroted half-heartedly.

They touched glasses, and Katie smiled wide before taking a long sip of her UrbanMech through the straw. Ramirez took her well whiskey all down with one gulp and slammed the glass upside down onto the counter like she'd just completed a challenge.

"Let's do this," Katie said before taking another slow sip of her drink.

"You might want to finish that before we go over there."

"Huh?"

Ramirez's face pushed tight with obvious impatience. "You can tell a lot about a person by what they're drinking. An UrbanMech doesn't exactly inspire confidence. You might want to finish it up before we head over."

"But UrbanMechs are delicious."

"Delicious, and still not confidence inspiring."

Katie harrumphed before taking another long, slow sip. The level of liquid in her glass slowly depleted, and she could feel it in her head. When she moved, her consciousness followed just a second behind her. The straw gurgled when the liquid vanished.

She slammed the drink on the counter with the same verve Ramirez had, but it didn't have the same oomph to it. She shrugged.

Whether her consciousness and body married in lock step, Katie had to talk to the broker, so to his booth she went. Ramirez followed close behind, and Katie liked the feeling of having Ramirez at her back. Someone she could trust. Naturally, the broker had chosen a spot where his back was to the wall and he could keep an eye on all the exits. Anyone who came to negotiate with him would have to leave their back exposed. But Katie had Ramirez.

It offered quite a lot of comfort, and Katie was starting to like the fact that Ramirez packed her pistol. Ordinarily Katie didn't like guns. She didn't feel comfortable around them. They made her feel unsafe, whether it was her wielding one or someone else. Just the idea that so much destructive power was around and she couldn't be safe inside her 'Mech unsettled her.

This was really the first time she found the presence of one soothing.

As Katie approached, she locked eyes with the nameless broker, and he invited her closer with nothing more than a look.

Then, when she and Ramirez came within comfortable earshot, he spoke in a deep, velvety baritone, in a subtle accent she didn't recognize. "Ah, you must be my next appointment."

Katie nodded her head. "Morgan sent me."

"Yes, yes, very good. Morgan's a very good friend of mine. Please, sit."

To Katie's knowledge, the Morgan in question had been dead for seventy-five years. Or, depending on the speaker, Morgan didn't exist at all. But it didn't matter; it was just a password. She sat down and stayed there, leaving Ramirez to stand behind her, staring down at the proceedings with her arms folded.

Katie had to admit Ramirez looked pretty intimidating.

The broker didn't even give Ramirez a second glance. He was probably so used to folks arriving with muscle and backup that they just became invisible to him. And he probably had muscle of his own scattered around every corner of the Broken Locust.

"Tell me about your unit," he said. "Because I think I have just the right job for you, depending on how you're outfitted."

"We've got a mixed lance of five 'Mechs. Two heavies, two lights, and a medium. We run in a converted *Confederate*-class DropShip, and we're nimble. We've got the best 'Mech technicians in the mercenary world, and we keep our equipment in tip-top condition. We've fought everything from Clan assault 'Mechs on down, and we keep winning. So if you've got anything a lance can help with, we've got everything you need."

He nodded with every word she spoke, taking mental note. On his face, writ large, were the calculations he computed in his head, which he tilted back and forth. "JumpShip, too?"

"No, just the DropShip."

"Hmm..." He made more mental calculations. "And who did you say referred you?"

Sweat beaded on Katie's brow. Was this some sort of test? "I was told no names. But she, uh, she said she did the Overstreet job for you."

It took a long moment, and Katie couldn't cope with the dread she felt in that pause, but eventually he smiled. "Very good. My clients value discretion, so we don't really use names if we can help it. Not here."

Ramirez cleared her throat. "If you don't know who we are, how do we get paid?"

Finally, the broker looked up and regarded Ramirez, but his smug smile never faded. "An excellent question. We'll arrange another meeting to exchange the information about your banking accounts and, at the same time, we'll deliver the packet of information about the assignment."

"So, there's an assignment?" Katie said, hopeful she'd done good. There was almost no way it could be this easy to book a job on Galatea. She didn't have to fight in a gladiator pit, and she didn't have to sell out the ideals of the Fox Patrol just to get some work. She did it right. She made the right contacts before coming, and things were easy.

She'd earned this.

A clattering behind her dropped that feeling of triumph from her chest and replaced it with concern.

She spun around to see what the commotion was. She figured it was a bad habit of hers she had to get out of, because if it wasn't her business, she shouldn't care. But she also needed to be aware of her surroundings.

The noise had been a barstool kicked over, and a woman dressed in black—or at least it looked black in the dim lights of the Broken Locust—marched in the general direction of the broker's table, gun drawn.

This woman looked nothing short of pissed.

Katie, looking back at the broker, then back to the woman, realized this *was* her business.

"Rolando," the woman growled, raising the pistol in the broker's direction.

He raised his hands. "Hold on now, I think there's been some sort of mistake. I know we can sort this out."

"The whole thing was a setup! You think we can really sort that out?"

"No, if something went wrong, we can—"

The broker—Rolando, apparently—never got to finish his sentence. By the time the woman reached the table, standing side by side with Ramirez, she fired her pistol. The slug hit Rolando in the left shoulder.

The report was loud, and Katie's ears rang. She could barely hear any of the panicked crowd around her. The gunshot had the instant effect of making everyone in the Broken Locust flinch. Then the smart ones by the door fled immediately; no drink in the world was worth staying for whenever shooting started.

Katie just sort of sat there, watching the broker she'd pinned her hopes to bleed. He grabbed his shoulder, covering his hands in blood. His jaw set tight, and Katie was sure he screamed, but her ears still rang too loud to hear it.

She knew the gun must have gone off again because she saw the muzzle flash once more, blinked, and then another leak had sprung in the broker; another hole. This time in his chest, right above the arm clutching his wounded shoulder.

Katie looked up to Ramirez, who didn't regard her at all. Her eyes were scanning the room as she gauged the situation. There wasn't really anywhere for her to move, and that trapped Katie in the booth as well.

The walls closed in on Katie. She felt tightened, under fire in a foxhole and looking for a way to jump over the wire in the other direction.

Panic rose in her, and she instantly hated herself for it. In her 'Mech, there would have been no question about it. She'd have known exactly what to do. Only in her own skin did she feel naked, no matter how clothed she was. Without the comfort of her *Kit Fox*, she had no idea what to do.

"God damn it," she said to herself. Even the sound of her own voice felt distant, underwater. She could barely hear it at all, only through the vibration she made when she spoke.

The ringing hadn't subsided, and everything felt so far away.

When the woman who'd killed the broker turned to Ramirez, Katie couldn't even fathom what would happen next. Would she take umbrage at their presence? Would she hold them responsible for whatever double-cross she'd blamed on the broker? Katie couldn't hear a word she said, but she was clearly upset and shouting something at Ramirez. Ramirez raised her hands in a nonthreatening way, trying to calm the woman down, but that seemed to have no effect. She spoke, too, though Katie couldn't make out what she said, and that didn't help either.

Slowly, sound seeped into Katie's understanding, then it came back all at once. She swallowed and yawned, hoping to bring it back further. It came back enough for her to function, but not soon enough to understand what Ramirez and the woman were arguing about. All she saw was Ramirez snap into action.

Ramirez did two things at once, fast. First, she slapped the gun from the woman's hand, and it clattered to the floor, sliding until it hit the wall. Second, she brought her foot up and smashed the woman's knee with her boot. The *crack* Katie heard, she couldn't tell if it was the gun hitting the floor or the woman's knee breaking.

The only sound she could track for sure was the woman's scream.

Ramirez grabbed Katie by the collar. "We gotta go!" she shouted as though she couldn't hear herself either.

And then Katie was on her feet and ready to run.

"Now *this*," Ramirez said, too loud and with a smirk, "is what I call a party."

Katie and Ramirez bolted for the door, but that didn't stop the woman. She hobbled toward her gun, and Katie could faintly make out the instructions she was shouting: "Get them! Don't let them get away!"

To whom the woman gave orders, Katie didn't know, didn't *want* to know. She just wanted to escape.

Katie's view was largely consumed by Ramirez, so at first she didn't see the man standing at the entrance. But he looked mean and ready to prevent them from leaving, no matter the cost. She didn't notice a gun, but when she heard another gunshot, she couldn't quite pinpoint the sound, as it echoed across the entire place. She looked back to find that the broker's killer hadn't retrieved her gun yet, then Katie looked ahead, realizing Ramirez had drawn hers.

At a full sprint, Ramirez wasn't as accurate as Katie would have hoped, and the guy in the doorway remained there, a bullet hole exploded in the plaster fresco, right in the face of a painted rendering of Grayson Carlyle.

"Whoops," Katie said, as though anyone could hear her.

Ramirez fired again, but they were too close. The heavy in the doorway knocked her gun away and leaned in with a nasty left hook. She seemed to intuit that move, though, because she tilted her head so the blow only glanced the side of her face. Using all of her forward momentum, Ramirez got low, almost as if to tackle him, but came back up with her knee and drove it into his groin.

He collapsed, clutching himself, and Ramirez jumped over him and turned, giving Katie a look that said, "*What are you waiting for?*"

Unsure, Katie didn't feel comfortable jumping over the downed goon. What if he reached up and grabbed her?

The bullet that whizzed by her head, shot from the woman at the back of the room, changed Katie's mind for her. She didn't hesitate for another second and took a running leap over the man, pulling her feet far enough above him so he couldn't easily grab her.

Landing on the other side, she felt relief until she heard another gunshot.

Not feeling hit and not wanting to wait around to see who or what *did* get hit, Katie just followed Ramirez up the street, opposite the direction they'd come. She only looked back once as they ducked into an alley, and saw the man hobbling after them, the woman bursting out of the Broken Locust, a bull escaping its pen. Turning and looking right at them, the woman had all the ferocity of a frenzied Jade Falcon hunting their prey.

"Run," Ramirez said to Katie. "Just run!"

And run they did.

GALATEA CITY
GALATEA
22 FEBRUARY 3149

Katie opened her eyes and felt like she hadn't slept a wink. The mattress was dodgy, full of broken springs. But that was what she and Ramirez got for holing up in a seedy motel on the wrong side of town, trying to hide from their pursuers.

Katie looked over to the other bed in the room. It looked barely slept in, and Ramirez wasn't in it.

"Rhiannon?"

Katie heard a rustle at the window and found Ramirez there. She stood stoic in front of the venetian blinds, separating two of the slats with her fingers at eye level, looking out for anything out of the ordinary in the cool dawn of the Galatean morning.

"Good morning," Ramirez said to Katie, quietly, as though speaking any louder might wake their pursuers or tip them off to their presence.

"Oh." Katie rubbed sleep from her eyes and slobber from her chin. "Good morning."

"You sleep okay?"

"You ever have one of those nights where you just sort of blink and you've time-traveled through to morning and you don't feel like you actually slept?"

"Yeah?"

"That." Katie yawned and sat up. The sheets were stiff, but she still pulled them up over her knees. She was too cold to want to get out from under the covers completely. "They still out there?"

"Don't know. I think we might've lost them. Or at the very least bored them."

"I hope we lost them."

"No one wants to be boring."

"I still can't figure out why they got so mad at us." Katie covered her ears, hoping she might be able to make some of her tinnitus go away. She uncovered them and covered them, back and forth, realizing there was no discernible difference between the two.

"It'll go away on its own," Ramirez said, as though she had experience with that sort of thing. "And they were mad at us because they didn't know who we were, and we were meeting with the folks who double-crossed them. We were natural targets."

"But you explained we didn't have anything to do with it."

"These people don't exactly seem stable. They murdered a guy in the open. It's not like they have the sort of political cover to get away with that. Which means they're desperate. And foolish. And capable of anything."

"So what do we do?"

Ramirez shrugged. "You're the captain."

"And I'm deferring to your superior experience. That's what captains do."

"Well, I say we wait it out. They can't stay mad forever. And soon enough, they *will* get bored. There are much bigger fish to fry on a planet like Galatea."

"Galatea," Katie repeated, wondrously. Even with her life in danger, she still managed to maintain her childlike awe of the planet. "If we survive this, this is going to be a story we tell."

"Will we? Because I don't think it makes us look all that great."

"No," Katie said, "you see, it's a great story. Here we are, on Galatea for the first time as a unit, looking for work—"

"—and we watch a guy get his brains blown out in a bar."

"He got shot in the chest."

"Point stands."

"Fine. Fair enough. But then we end up on the run from these loose cannons and spend a night in a seedy hotel trying to hide from them. It's sort of charming."

"You really didn't get off Jerangle until after you formed the Fox Patrol, did you?"

"No, but what's that got to do with anything?"

"Forget I said anything." Ramirez looked out the window again, keeping a sharp eye out for any ne'er-do-wells.

Anxious as she was, Katie kept telling herself versions of the story like they were in some sort of dark and shifty novel. They were the heroes on the run from the heavies, and any minute now, there would be a break in the case to let them turn the tables and win the day.

But the world didn't work like that.

Instead they waited.

And waited.

And waited.

Katie thought she would die of boredom. *That* was how the world worked. Boredom punctuated with the occasional spurt of excitement.

And checking her noteputer for messages, she didn't realize the excitement would be compounded.

"Oh, no," she said.

"What?"

"Oh, no," Katie repeated.

"What is it?" Ramirez actually sounded worried.

"The wedding."

"What about it?"

"Arkee and Evan are getting married."

"You said that."

"I know, but like…" Katie looked down to the chronometer on her wrist. It said 1722. "In like less than an hour."

Ramirez closed her eyes, annoyed. "You've got to be kidding me."

"No. The wedding is at 1800."

"They picked sunset?" Ramirez said, looking back out the window to check for any signs of danger. "Seriously?"

"Well, the message said it was the time the light through the rose window was the best. They're really into that sort of stuff, I guess."

"Of course."

"What?"

"There they are." Ramirez let the slats clack back together, then dropped to the floor, hoping they hadn't seen her.

"We can't miss the wedding, Ramirez."

"I'm sure."

"We're going to have to figure out how to get there."

"There are two goons out there with guns who are obviously willing to kill us. They're waiting for us for reasons we absolutely do not understand. You really want to go out there? For a *wedding*?"

"Arkee and Evan would do it for *your* wedding."

"First off, I'm not getting married. Secondly, they want to kill us, Captain."

"Well, they're not going to."

"How are you going to stop them? You going to just ask them nicely?"

Katie got back up, slid her noteputer into her pocket, and got up to look around the room. "There has to be another way out of here."

"Unless you think you can get out that half window in the bathroom, we're stuck here. We walk out the front door or not at all."

"I'm willing to try the window." Katie went into the mold-green bathroom, and the description "half window" was generous. It looked about a third of a meter, tops. And it was high up on the wall of the soap-scummed shower. The frosted glass hadn't been cleaned in ages. Ramirez definitely hadn't picked this place for quality.

The window itself slid open to the left, but the opening only exposed half of the outside. How would they get out? Squeezing wasn't going to work. It really was too small. Katie allowed herself to grin for a moment, though. Climbing out a bathroom window *would* have made a really great story.

She snapped her fingers together. "I got it."

"Got what?" Ramirez said. "If you've got an idea, now's the time for it."

"A diversion. We break this window and make them think we went out through here while we waltz out the front door instead."

"You're aware there's two of them, right? They can cover both exits."

"Well, dealing with one of them and distracting the other evens our odds, right? Putting at least one of them off-balance is going to help us more than anything. Right?"

"So what do you propose?"

"You stick close to the door, watch 'em. I'll break the window and think of something."

"*That's* the plan? You'll break a window and 'think of something'? Forgive me if I'm not inspired by your rousing leadership style and foolproof plan."

"It's going to work," Katie said, looking around for something she could use to shatter the window. There weren't really any objects in the bathroom that would do the job. Katie could have put a boot through the window if it were a lot lower, but that wasn't applicable in this case.

She rushed into the bedroom and looked around, finding a lamp, sitting on the side table, lighting the room. "Bingo." Wrenching the lamp off the table, she dragged it into the bathroom. "You ready?"

"Jesus Christ. As ready as I'll ever be. Let's just do this and hope they don't shoot to kill."

"It'll work. Trust me, Ramirez, it'll work."

Katie lifted the lamp high above her and took in a deep breath. The calm before the storm.

Glimpsing herself in the mirror, lamp raised above her head, face contorted into a fierce pose, Katie thought she embodied the very image of a badass go-getter. She'd certainly follow her.

"You can do this, Ferraro. You're a badass," she said to herself before growling in the mirror.

From the other room, Ramirez shouted loud enough for Katie to hear her, but hopefully quiet enough for the goons not to. "Will you just do it already?"

Katie steeled her resolve and shoved the lamp right through the glass. It shattered, but left plenty of shards still hanging. Gritting her teeth, she banged the rest of the glass out of the frame and then tossed the lamp into the alleyway behind the motel as hard as she could. It shattered against the wall on the other side, and Katie wasted no time returning leaving the bathroom.

Ramirez stood there at the window, trying to spy through the slats without opening them any further.

"Well, did it work?" Katie asked.

Ramirez raised a finger behind her, as if to tell Katie to keep her mouth shut.

"Did it?" Katie whispered, not knowing when to take a hint.

Ramirez hesitated, stone still, then said in a harsh whisper, "We gotta go. Now!"

Before Katie could even realize what was going on, the door was open and she and Ramirez had fled. Katie didn't stop to look when a voice shouted for them to stop. She just kept following Ramirez, hoping she would be able to get them to the church on time.

As they rounded the corner, Katie flinched at a puff of masonry and the trademark sound of a ricocheting gunshot, but never lost her momentum.

"This way," Ramirez said.

But to Katie, the streets seemed like a maze. She'd known where she was going in the first place; she'd had a map and looked up the layout. But when Ramirez had taken them to the motel through circuitous routes and alleys, Katie had gotten well and completely lost. Why couldn't her face have a head-up display like her 'Mech? At *Kagekitsune*'s controls, she'd get to the church in no time flat.

"Keep up!" Ramirez said, as though Katie were lagging behind. But she wasn't. Of course she wasn't. She couldn't. There was too much at stake, and goons were still hot on their heels.

Every so often, Katie would hear a shout or flinch at a gunshot.

Thank God their pursuers were such terrible shots. Not that most people could really hit anything with a pistol at that distance, running and out of breath, trying to hit a moving target. Maybe they'd get lucky, but more likely they would just kill a bystander, and no one wanted that.

Then she would glance down at her chronometer to see how far behind they were.

1750.

Then she blinked, winded.

1755.

They were never going to make it.

Ramirez rounded another corner with Katie close behind her, and there it was: The Archangel, majestic as ever as the sun set on that little patch of street. A golden shaft of light poured onto the rose window like honey, and they were this close to getting away with it, but their pursuers rounded the last corner in time to see Katie disappear in the direction of the church.

Another round of useless shouting for them to stop, the sound of more bullets firing at their feet.

Katie wondered how their pursuers still had the breath to scream, they'd all been running so hard. Her lungs burned and she could barely form words. How could the others do it?

Maybe they just had a lot more practice racing through the streets of Galatea, chasing down people they barely knew, loosely involved with people they hated. Was it because she and Ramirez had witnessed the murder?

Katie couldn't figure it out.

Were they fabled mercenaries, even? Or just anonymous goons? None of it made any sense. But Katie and Ramirez were going straight for their sanctuary.

The old wooden doors on creaking hinges swung outward, as if to welcome Katie and Ramirez. Surely the thugs wouldn't try anything inside of a church.

Right?

Katie glanced down at her chronometer.

1759.

God damn it.

She was going to miss it if they didn't hurry.

Blinded by the shift in light, Katie wasn't prepared for the Cathedral of St. Michael to be as dim as it was. They really went old school with the design, as though it had really been built in some Gothic period in the Terran countryside. But Arkee and Evan were right: the light coming through the rose window shone brightly on the two of them, right at the altar, standing in front of the bishop.

Ramirez and Katie absorbed all the cruel stares from those inside the nave. Fortunately, there weren't more than a dozen people inside, sitting scattered across the pews. Each gaze penetrated them, as if to say loudly, "*Sit down!*" and the organ music punctuated the need for them to sit.

Arkee and Evan, though, had relief writ large across their faces beside the happiness.

Katie couldn't tell if she wanted to glance behind her, to see if their pursuers had the audacity to enter and shoot up such a sacred place, or to focus on Arkee and Evan, each of them wearing...

"What the hell are they wearing?" Ramirez murmured, matching Katie's thoughts.

Their uniforms looked like they were en vogue a hundred years ago in Lyran space, replete with dangling sash, high collars, and shoulder fringe. Except the uniforms themselves were in Fox Patrol colors. Polite people would call them old-fashioned. Not-so-polite people would call them ridiculous. But it warmed Katie's heart that the Fox Patrol meant so much to them that they chose to incorporate it into their wedding.

It seemed the bishop herself, wearing the classic miter, was conducting the ceremony. As the organ music faded, she began the ceremony. Neither Arkee nor Evan were actually Old Catholic, though, so either the church was getting more broadminded or the couple had lied in their interview. Either way, the scene before Katie was the most beautiful thing she'd ever seen.

As the bishop began the ceremony, Katie looked behind to see their two pursuers calmly stroll into the church as though they owned the place. Their guns were safely holstered, and they looked around like tourists.

They took a seat in the back pew, and Katie couldn't even begin to know how to divide her attention. She just wanted watch the wedding ceremony, but people trying to kill her were sitting *right* behind her.

When the bishop finished the ceremony, Arkee and Evan embraced with a deep and passionate kiss. Claps erupted from the meager crowd, including the two wedding crashers, and Evan and Arkee turned back to the aisle then came toward them, hand in hand.

Evan caught Katie's eyes, and she tried to instill as much terror in them as she could, hoping to warn them of the danger they were in. Or ask for help. Somehow. Silently.

Realizing something was wrong, Evan broke from the normal, "get the hell out of the church" protocol and stopped at Ramirez and Katie's pew. He shook Ramirez's hand and embraced her, giving her a kiss on each cheek. Then he did the same for Katie. Arkee followed suit, hugging Ramirez behind Evan.

As Evan embraced Katie, she whispered close to his ear. "They're trying to kill us. We've been on the run. Help if you can."

Evan smiled. "I'm so glad you could make it to our special day."

"Me, too," Katie said loudly.

"We'll be off now," Evan said, hamming it up.

As though they weren't just leaving their own bloody wedding.

Katie and Ramirez turned around, facing the door, watching Arkee and Evan leave. The goons stood there, staring at Katie and Ramirez. Waiting for the coast to be clear. Waiting for them to make a move.

But they didn't have to.

Arkee and Evan cracked them both on the back of the head before they could draw their pistols again.

They crumpled to the floor.

Then Evan looked up Katie and said, "So what the hell is this all about?"

Katie shrugged innocently. "A wedding you won't forget?"

CONFEDERATE-CLASS DROPSHIP *FOX DEN*
GALAPORT
GALATEA
23 FEBRUARY 3149

"Are you serious?" said Frankie Fischer, the chief 'Mech tech for the Fox Patrol, listening to the entire story with their mouth agape as they made some adjustments to Evan's *Locust*. "*That's* what I missed?"

"It was sort of awful, Frankie, be glad you did," Katie said.

Watching Frankie work made her think back on the days when she would sit and listen to Scarecrow's stories as she helped him repair AgroMechs on Jerangle.

It felt like home.

Frankie went back to tooling a bolt on the inside of the control panel. "And the authorities just swept those thugs under the rug?"

"Well, the cathedral's security team, yeah. They detained us, too, but when we told them the story, it all worked out in the end."

"Who were they?"

"Mercs from another unit."

"Which one?"

"Doesn't matter. They're not the Fox Patrol."

"And are we going to find a job? We don't have much more time on the rental for this blast pit."

"I know, Frankie. We'll find something."

"We'll have to."

"We *will*," Katie said, more sure than anything in her life. They were the Fox Patrol, damn it, and they would weather this storm like they'd weather all the others. "We'll get a gig soon. I promise."

And she smiled.

For this was the life of a MechWarrior.

And she wouldn't trade it for the world.

FIVE
THE FOX HUNT

CONFEDERATE-CLASS DROPSHIP *FOX DEN*
ON APPROACH TO MORGAN'S HOLDFAST
TORTUGA DOMINIONS
8 JUNE 3151

For her 26th birthday, Katie Ferraro, the leader of the mercenary group known as the Fox Patrol, got herself a new mattress for her bunk and hired another member to her growing crew.

Their lance had held steady at five 'Mechs over the years. Technically more of a Star, as the Clans would say, but Katie didn't want to command from the DropShip—which had itself been completely retrofitted and overhauled.

Three years was a lot of time for a merc unit.

And it was even more time for a MechWarrior like Katie. She wasn't the most talented MechWarrior, but she'd learned a thing or two. She'd learned a lot about leadership and tactics. She'd also learned that the key to a good battle is less in the tactics and more in the logistics.

Things had gotten so much easier when she'd been able to hire a permanent crew for the *Fox Den*. That meant they were able to double as a ship's crew when DropShip was in the air and taking them from engagement to engagement, and then they could be her maintenance team when they were on the ground.

She trained them as hard as she drilled the MechWarriors in her outfit. In fact, Evan and Arkee—the first two mercs she had brought on—were convinced she was harder on the maintenance crew than she was the MechWarriors. Which suited them just fine. Since there were more hands around to do the work, they had more time to treat the time between missions as a permanent honeymoon.

Katie didn't understand how those two could remain so in love after everything they'd been through. After all the fights and arguments and battles. But they always made up. She didn't feel the same draw to people, men or women, like those two did. She just assumed it took different sorts of people to populate the entirety of the Sphere.

Her other two MechWarriors, Nicks and Ramirez, had tried dating once, back in '49, but that had ended poorly when she slapped him across the face at a dinner. There wasn't any real reason for it, she just thought it would be funny. And he really didn't like being humiliated.

Katie'd had to mediate between them for the entirety of 3050. He wouldn't speak to her, so she was the conduit between the two of them. The lunar patrol job was a lot of fun with that going on. They got over it eventually, though.

And she was glad for it.

They were all back to being one big family.

The *Fox Den*'s briefing room had been updated significantly. And by significantly, that meant a new table and much more comfortable ergonomic chairs, rather than the aluminum back-killers that were tossed in there by some sadist in the DropShip's past.

It gleamed with polish. The maintenance team took their cleaning rounds seriously. the *Fox Den* hadn't been a crumbling joke in at least a year.

She found the MechWarriors of the Fox Patrol waiting for her to arrive and give them their mission briefing.

Evan Huxley and Arkee Colorado sat together at the back of the room. Probably passing love notes to each other under the table.

Rhiannon Ramirez sat at the front of the class, as far away from Dexter Nicks as possible. With an internal sigh, Katie reminded herself that the situation between the two was better than it was—even if it still had room for improvement.

The viewscreen on the back wall came to life at her push of a button. She'd been forced to create actual briefing presentations on a noteputer instead of just winging them. It had certainly aided in her ability to communicate what she wanted to do.

And the presentations had helped her really understand *why* she was doing things the way she was doing them. It was amazing how much more brainpower it took to communicate an idea rather than to just have one.

"How is everyone?" she asked, sipping from her mug of coffee.

They all offered non-committal grunts. They never liked early meeting calls. Even though they had slowly phased the internal clocks of the *Fox Den* to more accurately represent the time zone of Morgan's Holdfast, it was still early for them. They slowly crept the time back so everyone would be fresh when they finally made their attack.

They hated it. But Katie found she loved it. Being up in the morning, walking around before the DropShip was awake, made her feel like she was pulling a fast one on everyone else. They said the early bird always got the worms, and Katie wanted to be the earliest hawk she could be.

"Well," she continued, forcing as much cheer into her voice as possible, "we've got a doozy of a job, let me tell you."

"We going to get stranded again?" Arkee asked, and the rest of them laughed.

This was the sort of outfit she'd cultivated.

"No. And I will kindly order you to never bring that up again."

"It's just hard to forget, is all."

"I understand that."

Ramirez rolled her eyes and let out a growl of a breath. "Will you two cut it out with the back and forth and just let us know what it is we're trying to do?"

"I'm glad you asked that, Ramirez." Katie turned to the screen behind her. It wasn't even a holo screen. Just a flat 2D display. Ancient technology. "This is going to be an infiltration mission."

"Like espionage?" Nicks asked. "Or smash and destroy?"

"Smash and destroy." Katie switched the slide to an aerial view of a monstrous looking complex. The widest shot showed it was set on a cascade of desert dunes beside a lake-like outlet to a raging river. It looked to be a half-dozen buildings and a landing strip that two DropShips called home. There were laser cannon emplacements on the roof, just large enough to make out in the blurry reconnaissance photographs.

"This is the base of the Queen Anne's Privateers, a pirate operation stationed on Morgan's Holdfast in the Tortuga Dominions. We are to land and destroy the base and any 'Mechs we might find there."

"The five of us are supposed to take down a pirate base?" Evan asked.

"I don't see the problem," Ramirez said.

It was exactly that sort of attitude that was why Katie had to patch up her 'Mech after every engagement.

Katie flipped to the next slide. "I know it sounds daunting, but the intelligence of the client suggests they will not be home, for the most part, when we stage our strike."

"Where will they be?"

"I'm glad you asked that, Nicks." Katie advanced to the next slide. "This is the settlement of Bearclaw on New Port Royal. They trade in a lot of illicit goods, as well as vital supplies pirates find tasty. Namely booze and replacement 'Mech parts. The Queen Anne's Privateers, apparently, have a pretty regular raiding schedule. The folks in Bearclaw thought it would be easier and less damaging to them if they hire two sets of mercenaries to deal with the threat."

"Other mercenaries?" Arkee said.

Katie advanced the slideshow again. There, a logo for a merc unit none of them would likely recognize. It was the silhouetted profile of a raptor with its claws reaching down for its prey. "These are the Sparrowhawks. They're an outfit that specializes in fighter screens and space missions. They'll be hiding at the pirate point for New Port Royal, waiting for the Privateers to arrive. They'll ambush the DropShip and harry it with fighters in the hopes of bringing it down. With any luck, they'll never even make it to the ground. While that fight is happening at New Port Royal, we will land on Morgan's Holdfast and tear their base apart."

"What resistance should we expect?" Arkee asked.

"Minimal, according to the intelligence. From the reports, they take every available 'Mech with them. They leave behind 'Mechs in the repair bay, but those should only be 'Mechs that aren't in fighting condition. We also have transponder codes from the folks employing us that will make it look like we're the returning Privateers. The idea is that we won't have anything to stand in our way. We crush it, remove their ability to make any war on the people of Bearclaw or anyone else in the future. It's really a good thing we're doing. Saving the universe. And then getting all that sweet, sweet salvage."

Nicks tilted his head. "I mean, are we sure about this? It seems like it could be a set up."

"Who would be setting us up?"

"These Queen Anne people."

Katie frowned. "I mean, why would they set us up?"

"I don't know. It just seems like all of our jobs seem to end in a set up. Least since *I* joined this outfit."

Katie shook her head. "That's not true."

"It *feels* true."

"Something feeling true and being true isn't the same thing. Anecdotes aren't data, Nicks."

"My gut is to be trusted, cap'n. Regardless of the data."

"That's nice, Nicks." Katie advanced to the next slide. A closer view of the beachfront complex. "We're going to be landing on one of their empty pads."

"They have two DropShips?"

Katie nodded at Evans. "Yes, that's what the intelligence says."

Evans folded his arms in front of him. "What happens to the other DropShip while they're off doing their marauding or whatever the hell it is that they do?"

"It stays there. It's not like you'd take an empty DropShip with you on a mission."

Ramirez raised a finger. "But what if they are actually running two crews, and that second DropShip is fully operational with a lance of its own?"

"It's possible, I suppose, but the client's intelligence states the risk of that is negligibly low. Their lineup of 'Mechs on their raids has been consistent across worlds according to the intelligence reports the folks from Bearclaw have given us."

Nicks raised a hand. Katie tried to ignore him, but he just started talking anyway. "With all due respect, sir, if it were a set up, they'd give us the intel that would make us think it *wasn't* a set up."

"Are you going to assume that literally anything I say is proof this is a potential set up?"

Nicks shrugged. "When the solution's in front of you, all of the information is going to add up to it."

"This is *not* a set up."

"We'll see."

Katie sighed.

Ramirez finished side-eyeing Nicks and looked back up to Katie. "How long until we drop?"

"We're heading toward Morgan's Holdfast now. We jumped in at the zenith jump point to minimize any chance of running into them during turn over. They should be long gone by now, but intelligence suggests that they primarily use the nadir point."

Nicks lifted a finger and an eyebrow, ready to speak, but Katie stopped him before he could.

"And no, that's not evidence of a set up."

Nicks shut his mouth and lowered his finger.

"We'll be well prepared," Katie said. "And everything will be okay. Frankie there is going to take us in nice and smooth. We'll land, carry out our mission, and not have any problems."

Frankie Fischer, the Fox Patrol's pilot and mechanic, had stood quietly at the back of the room the entire time. None of the MechWarriors paid much attention to them until Katie pointed them out.

Now they stuffed their hands in the pockets of their work coverall, stained in grease. "Yeah, I mean, they have some anti-DropShip weapons it looks like, based on the satellite imagery you've got there."

Katie keyed the presentation back to the photos in question.

"So," Frankie continued, "That could prove to be a little bit of a hot mess if the transponder codes don't work. We're in tip-top shape, though. Even if they do decide we're hostile, we'll almost surely make it to the ground. I calculated our rate of descent and the maximum damage output they could put out and really don't think they could punch through us fast enough. But that also means we're going to be dropping a lot faster than you all might like."

Nicks swiveled in his chair and raised a finger toward Frankie, but Katie interrupted once again before he could speak. "Still not a setup, Dexter."

He deflated again.

"Frankie, continue, please."

Frankie nodded. "Well, I'll drop us in as fast as we can. When we land, and it'll be a bumpy landing, have no fear, we'll kick the doors open, sure as anything."

"And that's when we all burst out. We'll take the drop itself in our 'Mechs rather than the bridge, observation room, or our bunks. Then we open up and let them have it. We just blast our way in our out, destroying everything."

"I don't know about you all," Ramirez said, rubbing her hands together like a supervillain, "but this sounds fun to me."

CONFEDERATE-CLASS DROPSHIP *FOX DEN*
MORGAN'S HOLDFAST
TORTUGA DOMINIONS
10 JULY 3151

Strapped into her beloved *Kit Fox* and waiting for them to begin their preposterously rapid fall to the planet, Katie felt the drop was anything but fun.

When the turbulence started, Katie couldn't quite feel it. With her *Kit Fox*—*Kagekitsune*—all fired up, its stabilizing gyros took care of most of the shake. But as they sped up, a boulder speeding toward the ground, the shaking intensified, and her stabilizers couldn't keep up. More than a tremor, more than a groundquake, it vibrated from the hull of the *Fox Den*, though the framework of the 'Mech, and right into Katie's command couch.

She wondered if she would get sick.

"Woo-hoo," Ramirez called out through the comm as though she was on an amusement park ride.

"Frankie," Katie said, trying not to puke, "What's our ETA for landing?"

But Frankie just laughed.

They'd only just begun their descent.

It couldn't have been too long, but however long it was felt like an eternity.

"They're opening fire," Frankie called out. "Taking evasive maneuvers and increasing speed."

Nothing about this filled Katie with confidence. And she wanted to smack Ramirez for finding this fun.

Katie didn't get motion sickness easily, but she was pretty sure she was motion sick. Her stomach swayed and her eyes couldn't focus on the horizon on her view screen. It was perfectly stabilized itself, but her head shook and vibrated so violently her eyes couldn't lock onto the target.

So she closed them, hoping that would help.

But that only increased a rising sense of tension from the bottom of her stomach and into her chest. She wished she'd taken some sort of drugs to cut down on this. Frankie had even suggested it, but like a fool wanting to look tough, Katie had refused.

"Idiot," she told herself.

"What was that, cap'n?" Arkee asked.

"Oh, nothing, nothing." She cursed at herself as soon as she remembered to turn the comm off. "Damn it."

That was all she needed. Her entire mercenary unit hearing her call herself an idiot.

Ugh.

The DropShip lurched with no word from Frankie on how it was going, Katie was grateful she didn't vomit all over her bare legs or cooling vest.

"There is nothing pleasant about this," she said, before realizing that might have been a mistake, too. In all the years they'd been making DropShips, had no one ever really figured out how to stabilize reentries? Or were they just unlucky in that the *Fox Den* had a problem with them?

Katie wished she had more experience with other sorts of 'Mechs and DropShips and everything else that swirled around the orbit of being a MechWarrior. Her experience was limited to

The Fox Patrol. Most days that was good enough. Other days, she thought she might be a better leader if she'd been a little more seasoned.

She was a kid when The Fox Patrol began.

Hell, I'm still a kid now.

"We're touching down now. Opening the bay doors on my mark."

Frankie paused there, and Katie wondered what the holdup was until ship rocked back and forth and then settled onto the pad. They weren't opening up until The Fox Patrol was planted firmly on the ground.

"Mark," their voice said, and the doors in front of Katie cracked open.

Surrounding her across the bay were the other 'Mechs of the unit. Evan in his nimble *Locust,* Arkee in his heavy *Quickdraw,* Ramirez in her *Marauder,* and finally Nicks in his *Griffin.* Each 'Mech was painted in the rusty colors of The Fox Patrol, and they looked like a helluva team.

She wondered what they'd look like when the door finally did open.

Would the techs of Queen Anne's Privateers quiver in fear?

Would they have gun emplacements ready to fire back when they discovered it wasn't their mates and comrades who had landed?

As she thought about that, she wondered if they should install emplacements like that inside the *Fox Den.* She couldn't quite imagine a situation where they'd need them, but she also figured the pirates they were attacking wouldn't imagine they'd need them in the first place either. Better to be prepared than sorry.

The door slammed open and Katie prayed there were no 'Mechs waiting on the other side to blast them. If the intelligence had been wrong, or if the pirates were more prepared than they were expecting, that would take the job from risky to impossible.

Crashing to the ground in front of them, the door opened.

"No 'Mechs. Please, no 'Mechs..." Katie whispered.

When she finally saw outside, elation hit her: there wasn't a single 'Mech in the bay. The client had been right.

"All right," Katie said with a smile, "let's move out. Weapons hot, free fire once you're clear of the *Fox Den*."

"Yes sir," came the voices of The Fox Patrol.

Hearing their voices bolstered Katie, and made her feel like they could accomplish anything. And, with this job, they would. They'd dismantle the pirates and their legend would grow.

Katie and Evan, in the faster, lighter 'Mechs, led the charge out of the *Fox Den*, stepping out into the light of the Morgan's Holdfast day.

Surprise was on their side.

As soon as her *Kit Fox* stepped onto the pad, a thrill ran up Katie's back. If she hadn't been seated in the center of an ever-warming 'Mech, she would have shivered. There was something exciting about being able to just tear into a complex with wanton abandon. If the reports from the client were accurate, the place was largely a ghost town when the Queen Anne's Privateers were out marauding. Aside from the scant skeleton crew, there wasn't really anyone here to get hurt. The Foxes would simply take the Privateers' base of operations from them.

Katie wondered how often mercenaries were supposed to think about the jobs they were doing. *Should* they put an undue amount of thought into who might get hurt by their mercenary actions? Or was that something unique to Katie?

Still, something about the whole thing felt like trouble.

It was all quiet. Too quiet.

She fired her lasers, cutting into the steel beams of the 'Mech bay. Evan's *Locust* did the same thing. They stepped out into a formation that let all five 'Mechs of The Fox Patrol get a shot and they began their work tearing the place down.

There was an unrestrained glee about the whole affair.

First the 'Mech bay roof toppled, and then several fires flared up as the melting steel framework started to consume the wooden portions of the edifice.

The anti-DropShip emplacements on the roof collapsed along with it as the lance continued dealing out damage.

It was fascinating to watch how much damage a 'Mech could do to something—anything—that wasn't as well-armored as a 'Mech. Walls fell as though the entire pirate installation was built of nothing more than cards.

Katie smiled.

But then Frankie's voice came over the radio. "Problem incoming, boss."

"What?" But Katie didn't even need to ask.

"I think we kicked over a hornet's nest, boss."

Katie directed her attention to the DropShip on the second landing pad, which had opened up completely. 'Mechs poured out with purpose, angry pirates gunning for The Fox Patrol.

"Eyes up, Foxes, we've got hounds on the hunt. We woke 'em up, and they're comin' for us." Scanning her viewscreen, she made the turn to move across the pads and engage the pirates. Her computer tagged the first 'Mech out as an *Orion*. At 75-tons, it was heavy, but old. *Orion*s were tough old bastards, though, and there was a reason they were still around in the galaxy. They were reliable workhorses and easy to work on.

Behind the *Orion* was a trio of *Spider*s. Again, old, but instead of heavy, they were light and incredibly mobile. As soon as they crested the door and could navigate around the heavier 'Mech, they leaped into the air on jump jets, quickly closing the distance between them and *The Fox Patrol.*

The last 'Mech to make it to the door was a *Locust*. Having looked at Evan's 'Mech for years, Katie would have recognized it immediately, even without the computer.

All of the Queen Anne's 'Mechs were painted in black with white details and the symbol of the Jolly Roger painted on all of their torsos.

Katie found that so predictable. *Why can't pirates ever be more original?*

Doing the math in her head, Katie found their odds to be not so bad. "I know we outclass them by a lot of weight, but they're still dangerous. Those *Spider*s can give us a lot of problems if we're not careful. The *Orion* is going to hit hard, too."

"Roger that, Captain," Ramirez said. "Best strategy?"

Options ran through Katie's head. Should they take out the *Orion* first and then mop up the light 'Mechs? Or chase the lights first and save the heavy for last?

The *Orion* was a heavy hitter. And if they could eliminate it first, the others would be easier to deal with. It would be close, though. And she had plans in mind for that *Locust* if they could take it down without hurting it too bad. Even if it was worth nothing more than spare parts, it would be good for them.

To accentuate the point, the *Orion* let loose with its LRMs, the, billowing smoke behind the missiles tracing a path across the battlefield. The missiles were clustered loosely and peppered the ground in front of Katie, spraying sand and dirt up to the knees of her *Kit Fox*.

"Focus on the *Orion*. Let the *Spider*s spin their webs while we do. Save the *Locust* for last."

"Looking for some salvage?" Evan asked, interested with a personal stake.

"You know it. Now let's get out there and do this."

"Got it, cap'n."

The 'Mechs of The Fox Patrol turned toward the 'Mechs of the Queen Anne's Privateers. The pirates got their shots off first, though. All three *Spider*s missed to the point where Katie wondered if something was wrong with their targeting systems. The *Locust* didn't get in place to get a good shot before the Foxes had shifted their positions. Only the *Orion* scored a hit.

"I *told* you all this was a set up."

Katie ignored him. *No sense in arguing with a man who's made up his mind.*

Instead, she let loose on the *Orion*. Katie hadn't planned on using her salvo of missiles during this mission. She'd been saving them, but as she thought about it, she realized she'd been saving them for *this.* The missiles corkscrewed across the sky, over the sands between landing pads, until they exploded in a cascade across the *Orion*'s armor. Then her laser shots covered the distance in a blink, carving glowing lines into the 'Mech's torso.

The *Spiders* landed hard and jumped again, getting even closer to the fray. They were going to be a problem sooner than later. But the Foxes' focus had to stay on the *Orion*, or it would tear them all apart.

Nicks got the next shot off, blasting the *Orion* with his particle projector cannon. The blue-white lightning ablated chunks of the heavy 'Mech's torso armor.

Evan flew by with his *Locust* and fired with his own laser and machine guns as soon as he slowed down to aim.

Ramirez missed completely, and Arkee didn't even fire.

"Arkee, what's going on?" Katie asked.

It seemed unlike Arkee. He was usually the cavalry that helped them mop up the end of any entanglement. For him to have missed the order and not fire at all didn't bode well.

"I'm having trouble getting my firing systems online, Cap'n." He hid the panic in his voice well.

But Katie could tell. "What do you mean? You can't fire?"

"Something's going on. Something must have shorted? Maybe I blew a fuse?"

"'Mechs don't just blow fuses that stop your weapons from working, especially if you haven't taken any damage."

"Maybe it's sabotage?"

No. Katie knew something else was going on. But it wasn't likely sabotage.

It was probably bad technical work. Bad repairs. A faulty wire. They'd been dealing with dodgy replacement parts all the time. Why wouldn't this case be any different?

As she added up the math, she realized if they didn't have the heavy *Quickdraw* fighting, they'd be outclassed. And if they were outclassed, there was every way they could lose this fight.

And for a mercenary, there was no real coming back from that.

You lose an engagement, that's one thing. You lose a battle where you came into someone's home and started blasting it down and the defenders are going to kill you and obliterate your 'Mech. There wasn't a whole lot of gray area there.

Katie didn't want to die.

She went through a mental checklist of the sort of systems that could cause a problem and realized there were a few things Arkee could do while he piloted his 'Mech. It's not like he had to be shooting anything right then.

"You reset your computer systems?"

"Affirmative. The computers reset, but it didn't cycle the weapons."

Katie paused for a moment, willing her 'Mech into a better position, wishing she could strafe easier and get in a better shot. As it was, she had next-to-no torso movement, so she had to form up on anything it was she wanted to hit.

The *Orion*'s lasers passed right by her and fizzled beyond in the empty sky.

"That was close," she said to herself. Then she keyed her comm back to Arkee and the rest of The Fox Patrol. "You reset the weapon systems specifically?"

"No. Where is that?"

"You have a number of systems at the bottom right of your command couch, to the right of your legs. There's a cage of computer systems there. You need to find the one blinking white rapidly. That should be your firing systems."

"Ok, I got that, now what?"

"There's a switch on it. It's behind a cage so you don't just accidentally trip it. Flip that switch, wait ten seconds, and flip it back on. I'll be here when you get back."

"What do you mean when you—" and then his voice went dead.

That hard reset would reignite his radio as well as his weapon systems. He was talking to the void and probably didn't even know it.

In ten seconds, he'd be back.

Hopefully, it wouldn't be too late.

Katie fired at the *Orion* again, dissolving another piece of its torso. How long could it stand? It had *a lot* of armor. But they were all scoring good hits. She hoped it didn't stand as long as other heavy 'Mechs they'd fought against in the past. Sometimes, it turned into an out and out nightmare.

"*Spider*s coming in hot," Ramirez said on the comm.

The light 'Mechs landed in the field right between The Fox Patrol and Queen Anne's Privateers, each one taking aim at Ramirez in her *Marauder.* With Arkee's *Quickdraw* not firing on them and the *Griffin* further back, it made sense that they'd go for the biggest, deadliest target as close to them as possible. They opened fire with their paired medium lasers, and all scored a few hits. The numbers spinning in Katie's mind about how expensive this job was going to be kept racking up.

The costs were never far from her thoughts.

That's what made her the captain.

"Status, Arkee," she called out, hoping his reset had worked.

"Still nothing."

"You've got your radio back, though, so that's something."

"I can't shoot anything. That whole system is just locked up."

Katie chewed her bottom lip, thinking fast. She kept moving her *Kit Fox*, hoping she could make a more difficult target for the *Spider*s on the off-chance they decided to attack her. She wanted to keep the *Orion* in her sights, though. They *had* to take the heavy 'Mech out first, especially since it had kept up its oppressive suppressing fire against her. Thankfully, it had been missing the lighter, faster *Kit Fox*, but all it had to do was tag her once and she'd be out of the fight.

Pushing the firing stud, Katie flensed more armor from the *Orion.* It had taken a pounding, but showed no signs of slowing down.

Sweat dripped from Katie's face. Her legs were wet with sweat. She felt it drip from her arms and moisten the controls beneath her hands. Her palms were just as bad. She couldn't tell if it was the rising heat or the tension.

She fired again at the *Orion* with her lasers, but her colored flashes of lethal light missed the mark. For its part, the *Orion* pivoted and targeted the *Marauder* as well, scoring a hit with their missiles, rippling across the front of the *Marauder.* Between that and the *Spiders* unleashing their hell of medium lasers, these damn pirates were going to kill Ramirez.

Ramirez fired back, but missed.

Again.

Nothing was going right.

"Ramirez, what's the problem over there?"

"Targeting's borked."

"What do you mean?"

"The whole targeting system is off. Pulling left. I'm trying to compensate."

Katie growled. The technicians she'd hired were cutting corners. That was the only explanation. There was a reason she liked doing it all herself. She never had these sorts of problems when she worked on a 'Mech.

"Then compensate, and let's take this *Orion* down."

"Roger, roger."

"Arkee. Status."

"What else have you got? Because I don't have anything to fire with."

Damn it, she thought. "Damn it."

"I thought the same thing."

"I need you to pull the control panel off the console that is in front of your left leg. In it, you're going to reset the master weapons switch."

"It's a breaker that needs flipping. It is just a fuse, isn't it?"

"Not now, Arkee. Get to flipping."

"Aye aye, cap'n."

The *Spider*s jumped again, edging closer to the *Marauder.*

Katie fired again at the *Orion,* hoping she could carve off enough armor to make a difference, but her shot went wide, terminating at the DropShip in the background. The laser didn't even score the armor of the Privateers' DropShip.

And that made Katie worry.

So far, the DropShip hadn't fired.

Were their weapons not operational?

Did they even have anyone to crew the guns?

Or were they scrambling right now to get to them?

Maybe they were trying to lure them closer before obliterating them completely.

"Fox Patrol," Katie called out, "let's pull back, a little further away. Don't get inside the firing arc of their DropShip."

Nicks called back, the voice of reason. "Sir, we're already in their firing arc."

"Then we pull back outside of it. Just in case."

"Aye, aye."

Katie looked over to Arkee's *Quickdraw,* hoping she'd see some sign of him firing back at the enemy, but his 'Mech just stood still. Darting past it flew the *Locust.* Evan stopped and fired at the *Orion,* carving armor from its arm.

The *Orion* ignored the *Quickdraw* and the *Locust* and pivoted. Smoke exploded from its left shoulder as a stream of missiles rocketed toward Ramirez's *Marauder,* peppering it with explosions, top to bottom.

Ramirez was left in good enough shape to twist her torso to the right and she blasted the *Orion* with both PPCs. Then Nicks came in with a third direct hit with his *Griffin*'s own PPC.

The *Orion* was a sturdy 'Mech, standing tall and proud; a sentinel of duty that had stood for half a millennium. But three direct hits to its torso from the PPCs were enough to boil off its front armor, leaving its internals exposed.

Katie saw a turn in the battle, victory close at hand. "Hit it! Now!"

But before any of her MechWarriors could get the opportune shot, the *Orion* fired back at the *Marauder,* its ER large laser slicing through Ramirez's armor across one arm and then into the torso.

Then, the black colored *Locust* stepped right into Katie's line of fire. It was a smart move if the pilot's goal was to protect the heavier 'Mech so it could make harder hits against the Fox Patrol. It was a completely foolish move if the *Locust* pilot wanted to live much longer.

As badly as Katie wanted that sweet, sweet salvage, she smashed the firing stud on her lasers, carving a smoking heap of *Locust* leg armor right off the 'Mech like a turkey.

It wasn't enough to take the damn thing down, but enough that it would feel it.

Evan fired at the enemy *Locust* as well with his medium lasers, cooking off armor from the cockpit. Then Ramirez fired and her lasers aimed true, scoring a direct hit.

"Yes!" Katie shrieked as the *Locust*'s posture collapsed and it seemed to power down.

They hadn't hit it *that* hard. Evan's *Locust* would have taken at least a few more hits than that.

But it didn't collapse.

It just stood there, a 'Mech statue.

In the way.

Blocking her shot to the *Orion.*

She *could* fire at the *Orion*, but the last thing she wanted was to risk missing and hitting Evan with friendly fire. Aside from being bad form, she would *never* live it down.

Arkee was the furthest on the flank, and unencumbered by the *Locust* in his firing arc.

Of course, he was the one who didn't have any weapons.

"Yee-haw!" yelled Arkee Colorado through the comm.

Katie blinked and her eyes darted to the *Quickdraw* just in time to see it fire its entire battery of lasers at the *Orion.* She couldn't see the all of the aftermath, though. The *Locust* still obscured just enough of her view.

"Well?"

"Well what?"

"Did you *hit it?*"

"A bit."

"What do you mean a bit."

"One out of four ain't bad."

Katie had to stop herself from screaming.

"At least I *have* weapons operational." Arkee took the words right out of her mouth. *At least...*

"Do better next time. We can't take much more of this. Especially if the DropShip starts firing."

"Only a matter of time, Captain," Nicks said. "Thanks to the transponder, their response is slowed, but they're no doubt at battle stations by now. They'll be raining hell on us all any second now."

"That's just great. Continue pulling back. We'll put the *Fox Den* between them and us." Katie pedaled backward herself. "Ramirez, how are you doing?"

"These *Spiders* won't leave me alone. They don't hit very hard and never the same place twice, but it's starting to add up."

"Got it. Arkee, finish the *Orion.* Evan, Nicks, let's focus on the *Spiders* and give Ramirez some breathing room."

"Aye," they all said in unison.

Katie never tired of watching orders go out to her MechWarriors and see them executed almost instantaneously. It was like she was in control of five 'Mechs instead of just one.

And like very heavy puppets on very large strings, they reacted to her plan.

Ramirez, in the *Marauder,* stepped back and fired at the *Spider* right in front of her with her medium lasers and PPC. That *Spider* was the center of the trio hopping around and making themselves a nuisance. When the trio of beams hit it, the center of its chest just melted and suddenly the inner structure of the *Spider* lost integrity. Its head sagged into its exposed torso, and the pilot just wobbled in it, back and forth.

All Katie could do was thank her lucky stars.

Evan switched directions and ran for the remaining two *Spider*s. Nicks pivoted to get another *Spider* in their firing arc and let loose with his PPC. A flash of white-azure light cooked off an arm, shearing it entirely from the 'Mech.

Katie couldn't help but smile.

When the Fox Patrol 'Mechs all worked, they *worked.* They were a pretty good team, too.

She liked who she had around, though a couple of them maybe got on her nerves on occasion. And she was definitely going to have it out with the Fox technicians. They were way out of line, sending them into battle with malfunctioning 'Mechs.

That was life or death stuff.

Katie marched backward, but tried angling herself so that she could get a shot on the *Orion* past the *Locust* without risking a hit against Evan, but didn't feel good taking the shot. Since none of the *Spider*s were in her firing arc either, she didn't feel like she had any good shot to take. It was the one thing she hated about her 'Mech. Most of the others could pivot their arms or swivel their torso to line up a shot, but Katie had to aim practically with her whole 'Mech. Sure, the computer did its job with targeting, but she had to get the firing arc right first, otherwise nothing else mattered.

Add some cover in the way and it was over. There was nothing she could do.

"Where we at on the *Spiders*, Ramirez?"

"I got tagged again. They're small, but they bite nasty."

"I never liked spider bites. Do what you can." Katie turned her attention to Arkee, now that he had a solution on the *Orion.* "Arkee, what's the scoop?"

"Locking on again, now. Bastard is trying to pivot away and show me his back."

"Get him before it's too late."

"Working on it."

"Nicks, Evan, continue with the *Spider*s. Let's get Ramirez out of that web."

"*Aye, aye,*" they both said at the same time.

Yep. They're a pretty great team.

Satisfied, Katie grinned—until the DropShip finally opened fire.

It was just a single laser blast to start, a miss, too. But it sprayed sand high into the air, though most of the sand it hit melted right into a glassy surface across the dune.

Katie's eyes widened. "Take your next shot and let's get to the other side of the *Fox Den* ASAP." She switched frequencies to talk to Frankie aboard their own DropShip. "Frank?"

"We saw it."

"Anything you can do? We can use the help out here."

"I can try."

"Don't try. Do it. We're not going to last long with that DropShip firing on us."

"Understood, Captain."

The lasers aboard the *Fox Den* weren't automated. Maybe they were at one time on the ship, but to get them working at all, Frankie had been forced to rig them up to a firing console not on the bridge of the vessel. It wasn't ideal, but nothing in the life of a mercenary was. Their firing arc also wasn't always up to standard.

But Katie knew Frankie would do their best. They always had. If there *was* one person on the maintenance crew Katie could trust, it was them.

Katie took one more shot at a *Spider*—it flew wide and missed—before turning completely, doing her best to just turn around and book it away from the engagement zone as best she could. There was no sense in staying.

"Regroup," she called out to everyone, as though she hadn't already given the order. "Get out of here."

Mainly, she didn't want to suffer any more damage than they had to.

She couldn't afford to lose a 'Mech. Or a pilot.

"Another *Spider* down," Evan called out.

"Got the last one," Ramirez said.

With the *Spider*s out of action, Katie felt like she had permission to breathe a little easier. They could make it through this. "Arkee, Nicks, status? You coming home?"

"Working on it, Captain," Arkee said. Sounded like he was in trouble, though.

"I took the long way around," Nicks said. "Figured it would give them something else to shoot at."

As far as plans went, it wasn't the worst. But there wasn't any reason for Nicks to take the initiative to split the party. There was nothing intelligent about that. If the *Orion* decided to pursue, he'd be alone. And if there were other Queen Anne's reinforcements in that quadrant, he'd be toast.

But it was too late to have him come back. He'd end up running through the entire gauntlet by himself, the only target in sight. They'd swarm him, bees attacking from their broken hive. Each missile a stinger. Every laser a reminder that their honey was not free.

On her quickened march back around the *Fox Den*, Katie surveyed the wreckage they'd already wrought, but there was so much more work to do. They couldn't dally. They needed to neutralize the rest of pirate 'Mechs, destroy the rest of the base, and get the hell out of there before anyone else arrived to jeopardize her merc unit.

"Any resistance on the other side, Nicks?"

"Negative, Captain. It's clear sailing on the sand over here."

"Thank goodness for small miracles, at least. Get over here now."

"Yes, sir."

"Frankie, what's the targeting solution like on these 'Mechs?"

"Working on it, Captain."

"Not good enough."

"Understood, Captain."

Katie took two laser hits to her rear quarter as she ran, but fortunately they weren't from the DropShip and they hit the most heavily armored part of her *Kit Fox*, right in the torso region. She never knew if she should call it a torso or a head. On a *Kit Fox*, it was all pretty much the same thing. Whatever she wanted to call it, she couldn't take a shot like that again. One more and they'd be inside to her internal systems.

"All right, foxes," Katie said, sidling her *Kit Fox* up next to the far side of the *Fox Den*. "We've got one more operable 'Mech out there, which shouldn't be a problem. It's already had all its torso armor blasted off good. One well-placed shot and a stiff breeze will knock that heavy down. The real problem is that DropShip. And it's a big problem. It has the potential to sink this whole operation. Now, we need to figure out a way to take it down."

"Or take it over...?" Evan asked tentatively.

"That would be great, but I don't see that as an option right now. It's the only thing standing in the way of us completing our mission and getting the hell out of here."

Arkee's voice came in over the radio. "I don't want to break up the party, but that *Orion* is falling back, and I don't get the idea he wants to fight us as is."

Katie cursed under her breath. She had hoped the *Orion* would just follow them around the DropShip to their doom.

"So what have we got?" she said. "We've got an *Orion* camping in the firing zone of their own DropShip. And we need to at least take it out before finishing our work here. Right?"

"A question, sir," Ramirez said.

"Yes, Ramirez?"

"Who's to say it doesn't just head into orbit? The 'Mech bay is a lost cause for them at this point. And we could probably finish the rest of the base with the DropShip, nice and warm inside the protection of the *Fox Den*. Why would we need to bother finishing them off?"

"Because the whole point of this is to wipe out the capability of the Queen Anne's Privateers. Completely. I know this wasn't *exactly* in the scope of our contract, but the spirit of it is. And I wonder if we can get some sort of bonus for this if we're able to take it down. Their intelligence didn't suggest a second DropShip, so even *knowing* about it is valuable. We just need to be able to get off this rock to do something about it."

"Sir," Arkee, usually a voice of reason, said, "I wonder what Frankie might be able to come up with. If the two DropShips are at a standstill because of some sort of unspoken truce of mutually assured destruction, that means we get stuck here if we don't make the first move definitive, right?"

"That is a fair assessment. But what pirate was ever afraid to fight to the death?"

"Well, that *Orion* pilot for one," Evan said.

"Are their techs and DropShip crews pirates?" Arkee called back. "I mean, would our crew fight to the death?"

"I think pirates sign up to do piratey things, even if it's just fixing the 'Mechs. Maybe they do it in eye patches, though," Nicks mused.

"Or maybe their guns aren't working. Like ours. Maybe there's a reason this DropShip is here. Maybe they planned on taking it, but it was inoperable."

Katie considered it. A very real possibility.

She wished she knew for sure. Decisions were always made easier with *actual* information rather than suppositions. Guessing was a bad thing to have to do in battle. Such was the burden of leadership.

She bit her lip, debating her choices...

There was really only one sensible option. Or only one option, at least. She wouldn't cop to it being sensible. But they needed to do something. And what she came up with seemed like the only reasonable thing to do.

Okay, maybe not reasonable.

It was a thing to do.

"Okay, here's what we do. Evan, get to the other side of the *Fox Den.* Regroup with Nicks there. On my mark, we're going to swarm them. We'll all gun it and open fire on the engine thrusters or one of its landing footpads. We just need to keep it on the ground and do enough damage to make it very expensive for them to get that bird back in the air. Frankie, do what you can to open fire. Turn the *Fox Den* if you have to, but do it. We'll hit them with everything we've got."

"I'd suggest the engine thruster," Frankie said. "If they lose a footpad, they can still take off if they fire up the engines before they fall over."

"Good, I like it. Go for the thruster."

When she heard no voices of dissent, she figured she was on the right track. They'd just need to move fast.

Katie let out a long, slow breath. "Okay. Everyone ready?"

Their "yeses" chimed in over the comm one at a time.

"Mark."

Katie pushed the *Kit Fox* forward, gunning her engine and pumping the 'Mech's legs as fast as she could. The *Kit Fox* wasn't as fast as Evan's *Locust,* but it still covered a lot of ground pretty quickly. She'd made modifications on it to see if she could push it faster, but physics were physics.

The *Orion* opened fire from the safety of the Privateer's DropShip as soon as they rounded the corner. The shot came for Katie, since she led out first.

Good. That means he probably doesn't see Evan and Nicks on the other side. Better to blindside him.

All it would take was one more shot to the *Orion's* torso to take it out. It couldn't be *that* hard.

The *Orion* wasn't the only 'Mech shooting, though. The DropShip opened fire as well. The ground in front of Katie erupted with a laser blast, sand flying everywhere. A miss. A near-miss, but a miss nonetheless.

Katie lined up a shot with her lasers and fired, but the only thing she managed to do was melt off scaffolding in the 'Mech bay behind the *Orion.*

Nicks fired a volley of his LRMs, each missile spiraling toward the DropShip's engine. An explosion erupted at the top lip of the engine itself. Then more missiles smashed against it. Katie couldn't tell through the acrid smoke whether or not Nicks had done much damage, but he hit it nonetheless.

"Keep going! Make hard targets for the DropShip!" Katie said, juking back and forth with *Kagekitsune,* doing her best to befuddle the gunners.

On her screen, in the periphery, she saw Ramirez and Arkee following close behind, jagging back and forth. As soon as Arkee cleared Katie from his firing solution, he let loose a battery of missiles from his *Quickdraw's* LRM-15, smashing against the DropShip.

But she still didn't know how operable the *Orion* still was.

In a flash, she had her answer.

A salvo of missiles flew through the smoke, coming straight for her.

"Damn it!" Katie watched them come. Almost in slow motion. Right for her.

And there was nothing she could do about it.

Katie flinched on impact. The missiles hit one after another, scattered over the body of her *Kit Fox.* The explosions rocked her back and forth across her command couch.

When the smoke cleared, she found she couldn't move forward anymore.

Kagekitsune was shutting down.

Katie wasn't sure what she could do under a shutdown. Would her radio stay operational? Or would she be forced to watch everything in silence? Would her viewscreen stay on, or would she just sit there, quietly in the dark?

The power dwindled.

The lights winked off one by one.

And then, finally, Katie lost her viewscreen, too.

"Damn it," she said again.

She closed her eyes and took in slow, deep breaths, trying to calm herself. She wondered if she could affect the outcome if she *felt* hard enough.

But that was absurd.

Good wishes only ever got people killed.

MechWarriors lived and died by their skill and their cunning, not how good they felt about an engagement.

The sounds outside were muted through the *Kit Fox*'s armor. Things sounded differently when all the mics and speakers of the communication systems were off. Things were muted further through her neurohelmet. Katie debated taking it off, but there was every chance that she could get the 'Mech back online for at least a few maneuvers.

Explosions outside sounded distant.

Occasionally, she could feel the push of an explosion or the repeated ting of autocannon slugs impacting on something.

She couldn't smell much but the ozone of her own cooling reactor inside the *Kit Fox*. Since her 'Mech had been disabled, there was likely no reason to think she was still a target worth attacking. Which helped. The last thing she wanted was to just be murdered in an inert 'Mech.

But her worry grew for the rest of the Fox Patrol.

Were they operating at full capacity without her steady voice to guide them?

Or was it a mess out there?

Had Frankie been able to come up with a solution to destroy the other DropShip?

The unknowns were what killed her. And the helplessness. Suddenly, she was a kid in the jungle, sitting in a dark, inoperable 'Mech. She'd just washed her hands in the river after stripping a mummified MechWarrior of all of its trappings and burying it, but she could still smell it in the 'Mech. But it was quiet and dark.

Then, all she could think about was the possibility of the 'Mech. It was hers. She would be able to fix it and live her dream.

Now, all she could think about was how this might be the end of everything. With wrong wrong hit to her *Kit Fox,* her dream had become a nightmare.

Katie's stomach tightened and sweat beaded down her brow. Her foxes were out there by themselves. They were getting shot at, staring down the barrel of a DropShip and a pissed off *Orion.* Maybe more reinforcements had arrived. She didn't know. She couldn't know.

And that pissed her off even more.

But all she could do was sit.

And wait.

And she hated waiting.

What felt like an hour passed.

Or a day.

For Katie Ferraro, it was hard to tell.

It could have been less than five minutes. She'd tried to restart her 'Mech twice and she couldn't figure it out. She was starting to think she had a saboteur on the maintenance team, but she knew that was absurd. Never chalk something up to sabotage that could be easily attributed to incompetence. She was just going to have to work harder at training everyone on the crew and she was going to go back to working on *Kagekitsune* herself.

Locked in the dark with nothing but the echo of the fighting outside to keep her company, Katie wondered if she should crawl out on her own or wait until the battle was over. There was less than nothing she could do, running around on the battlefield in nothing more than her cooling vest. She kept a pistol in her cockpit, in case she needed it. But if she was using her pistol against an *Orion* or a DropShip, the battle wasn't really winnable anyhow.

At least here she still had some modicum of protection. Out there, one stray laser and she'd be vaporized into nothing.

Katie told herself she would get out and see what the situation was as soon as she could count to more than ten before another explosion sounded. At least then, things would have been more settled, and she'd probably be in less mortal danger.

That's what she told herself, at any rate.

When the circumstances finally met her criteria, she unbuckled from her command couch, pulled off her helmet, and came around to the hatch.

As soon as the first seam of daylight cracked through the edge of the door, she felt the cool ocean breeze of Morgan's Holdfast. Suddenly, the swampiness of *Kagekitsune's* cockpit didn't feel so oppressive, and that feeling only grew as she opened the hatch wider. Though the sun was high, it couldn't quite cut through the cloud of dust and acrid smoke she saw. The glimpses of the *Fox Den* she was able to make out through the haze gave her the impression it was still in one piece. Or at least remained in very large pieces.

Then, she climbed out further, peeking her head in the other direction over the top of her *Kit Fox.*

The sight before her caused her to blink once. Then again.

She couldn't believe it.

The Queen Anne's Privateers' DropShip was smoking from the engines and listing over due to a missing foot pad. They'd done both. A pillar of black smoke curled up above the DropShip. The pirates on the DropShip were evacuating every way they could, arms raised in surrender.

Katie climbed up even further, standing on top of her *Kit Fox.* Looking around, she searched for all the 'Mechs in her cadre, hoping none of them had been as badly damaged as hers.

On the far end, she was positive she saw the outline of Nicks' *Griffin* and Evan's *Locust* at the edge of the haze. They were both moving away from the enemy DropShip and speeding back toward Katie and the pirate facility beyond her.

Then she looked to the other direction.

Ramirez had her *Marauder*'s back to Katie, but it didn't look any worse for wear.

On the far side of Ramirez stood Arkee in his *Quickdraw*. It looked like the two of them had dealt some killing blows, as they were still facing the disabled heap of a DropShip. Behind them was the crumpled wreckage of the *Orion*, intact enough for her to start adding dollar signs to her thinking about it.

"Get to the base and finish it off," she said, forgetting she wasn't tied into any comm system and couldn't give any orders at that moment.

But they knew what to do.

Ramirez and Arkee both turned to face the complex.

Arkee would have taken up the call. As much as Evan wanted to assert himself as the second in command, Arkee was the designated second. As soon as Katie disappeared from the comm chatter, he would have taken over. She guessed the DropShip hadn't stopped firing when the engine had been blown, so they went for the foot pad. Frankie must have helped with the *Fox Den*, too, judging by some of the gashes in the fuselage. Frankie would have worked out some sort of situation that would destroy the DropShip.

Katie wondered as she watched her lance of 'Mechs move on to the original first phase of their mission, as if the Privateer's DropShip had already been compromised before they arrived, or if Frankie had devised some unorthodox strategy to obliterate them. In either case, she didn't care. She was just glad they'd prevailed enough to make it to the next phase of the operation. Or enough to resume the first phase, rather.

But if the information they'd had about there being no resistance was wrong, what else could be off? Could the other DropShip, full of their best 'Mechs, be that far off? Could the Sparrowhawks have failed in their mission? Or sent them turning back? Even if the other Privateer DropShip turned around, it would take a while to get back to them.

Time was precious.

They just needed to finish up and get out of there before the next blade fell on them.

Katie coughed in the smoke and wiped her eyes, looking around at the wreckage surrounding her. There was a lot of work to do if they wanted to get out of there with her *Kit Fox* and any other salvage.

They were going to have to move quick.

Climbing down *Kagekitsune,* Katie was a kid again.

She hoped that rush and exhilaration never left her as long as she called *Kagekitsune* her own. It felt like yearning dreams fulfilled, and made her eyes tear up in joy.

But she couldn't wallow in her nostalgia. She had too much to do.

As soon as her feet touched the ground, she sprinted toward the *Fox Den.* Her breath soon came in pants from running, and her legs burned. There was always an added weight to walking when you got out of a 'Mech that she was never quite ready for the gravity of a planet. When you added the sand to the equation, it felt like her legs might fall off from the effort. But Katie never stopped moving.

Climbing up the cargo ramp, Katie ran into the 'Mech bay.

"Frankie!" she called out. "Let's get a move on!"

She was going to need a *lot* of help.

CONFEDERATE-CLASS DROPSHIP *FOX DEN*
EN ROUTE TO GALATEA
18 JULY 3151

It took an hour they didn't have to get *Kagekitsune* up and running enough to get it into the *Fox Den.* The trouble urned out to be a faulty circuit that had gotten knocked out by the missile impacts, and Katie would need to reinforce it so it didn't happen again. While she spent time getting the *Orion* and the enemy *Locust* together as part of their salvage, Frankie went to work grabbing as much from the Privateers as they could.

At the end of the very long day, they wound up with quite a bit of salvage, which wasn't something they'd expected. They also got some recruits. Some of the pirates offered to join the Fox Patrol rather than suffer the consequences of remaining part of Queen Anne's outfit. They were eager for the chance to get away, and Katie would be happy to just forget they had fought against them. She'd just be sure to keep them far away from the 'Mech bay.

According to all the intel, they shouldn't have seen anyone at the base but a skeleton crew, not a fully operational DropShip and a backup lance.

But they did.

Katie knew she'd have to do better at thinking of contingencies.

Every day as the impossibly young leader of a mercenary unit was a learning experience.

The other big thing Katie learned was that she needed to work her 'Mech techs a lot harder. They'd gotten lazy and complacent. There was no other way to explain the abject failures during the engagement on Morgan's Holdfast. It should have been a milk run, and it would have been without all the mechanical mistakes.

Once they were safely off-planet, she spent most of the time on the DropShip in the 'Mech bay, repairing the Fox Patrol's 'Mechs.

She could almost hear Scarecrow's voice excoriating her for keeping her 'Mechs in such disrepair. Her *Kit Fox* had been a gift, and she hadn't been kind enough to it. So she *had* to fix it. Personally. Especially if everyone she'd hired was incompetent.

"Hand me that spanner," she said to her astech. But in her mind, she heard Scarecrow saying it with her.

Floating underneath the arm assembly for *Kagekitsune*, taking in the scents and sensations of the 'Mech, and just basking in the meditative nature of the work, Katie forgot to re-explain everything she was doing to the astech. She just got lost in the task.

"Sir?" a voice said after a long minute.

Frankie's voice. *What are they doing here?* "Frankie?"

"Yeah, I got somethin' you're gonna want to see, Captain."

Katie gracefully floated out from beneath the arm assembly. She couldn't read Frankie's face. Was that stoicism containing excitement or hiding fear? "What've you got?"

"Well, we got the message download, and there's something you're going to want to take care of."

"Can it wait?"

"Not if we want to make our window planetside."

"Window?" Katie stood up. Her brow furrowed and she wiped the grease from her hands with the rag that dangled from her hip. "We get a job?"

"Something like that."

Frankie handed the noteputer over to Katie and she read. At first, she assumed there must have been some mistake. Or maybe it was a prank. But it was all legit.

"You're kidding me?" she said to Frankie.

"It all checks out, Cap."

"Well, I'll be damned."

"What is it, sir?" the chastened 'Mech tech in the corner asked.

Katie's face soured. "Terra has fallen."

"Fallen? To who?"

"Clan Wolf."

"Holy smokes."

"There's more." Katie closed the noteputer, a sly grin on her face. "There's a hiring frenzy on Galatea. Lot of places are putting out work. And somehow, we made the list of invites."

Frankie grinned and folded their arms. "We gonna do it, boss?"

Katie smiled and nodded.

The Fox Patrol had made it to the big leagues.

Now they just had to make it count...

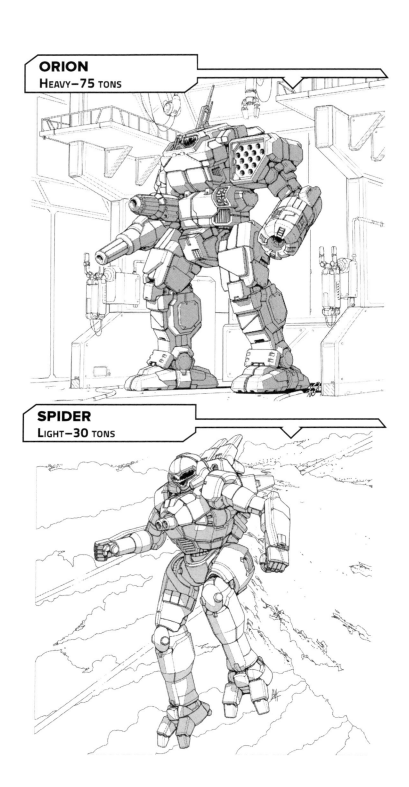

ORION
HEAVY—75 TONS

SPIDER
LIGHT—30 TONS

ACKNOWLEDGMENTS

This book would not be possible if not for a number of people. First and foremost, my family for allowing me the time and space to write. My wife Patty, my best friend Dawn, my kids—Anakin, Scout, and Valkyrie—all endure a lot for me to write, and I will always be grateful for it.

Then, Michael A. Stackpole for telling me to just write that first story in the first place and not wait for permission. I think it turned out okay. But I also owe Mike for his friendship and mentorship. He's a great guy, and doesn't deserve the flak he gets for that whole Stackpoling thing.

The editors in the *BattleTech* universe and of these stories in particular, John Helfers and Philip A. Lee, are owed much. They believed in these stories and printed them when I thought for sure they would turn them down. I think they ended up pretty popular—at least popular enough for a collection. If not, they've allowed me to fool them completely, and that's a reason to thank them, too.

My writing group, the Salt City Genre Writers, deserve a lot of credit for this, too. They have been a rock solid foundation for encouragement, notes, and community and I think that's something every writer named Bryan Young needs.

All of the *BattleTech* fans and fellow freelancers on Discord have been an invaluable resource as well, particularly the folks in the very inclusive Star League server. They're a great bunch, and really know their *BattleTech*.

There are hundreds of other people who deserve credit for helping me as I wrote these stories, but they would be too numerous to list. So if you didn't see your name specifically in print, know that I am still grateful. Yes, you. Especially you. You know you're important. Message me and I'll drop your name in the next one if I can.

ABOUT THE AUTHOR

Bryan Young (he/they) works across many different media. His work as a writer and producer has been called "filmmaking gold" by The New York Times. He's also published comic books with Slave Labor Graphics and Image Comics. He's been a regular contributor for *The Huffington Post*, *StarWars.com*, *Star Wars Insider* magazine, SYFY, /Film, and was the founder and editor in chief of the geek news and review site Big Shiny Robot! In 2014, he wrote the critically acclaimed history book, *A Children's Illustrated History of Presidential Assassination*. He co-authored *Robotech: The Macross Saga RPG*, and has written two books in the *BattleTech* Universe: *Honor's Gauntlet* and *A Question of Survival*. His latest book, *The Big Bang Theory Book of Lists* is a #1 Bestseller on Amazon. He teaches writing for *Writer's Digest*, *Script Magazine*, and at the University of Utah. Follow him on Twitter @swankmotron or visit swankmotron.com.

BATTLETECH GLOSSARY

AUTOCANNON

A rapid-fire, auto-loading weapon. Light autocannons range from 30 to 90 millimeter (mm), and heavy autocannons may be from 80 to 120mm or more. They fire high-speed streams of high-explosive, armor-piercing shells.

BATTLEMECH

BattleMechs are the most powerful war machines ever built. First developed by Terran scientists and engineers, these huge vehicles are faster, more mobile, better-armored and more heavily armed than any twentieth-century tank. Ten to twelve meters tall and equipped with particle projection cannons, lasers, rapid-fire autocannon and missiles, they pack enough firepower to flatten anything but another BattleMech. A small fusion reactor provides virtually unlimited power, and BattleMechs can be adapted to fight in environments ranging from sun-baked deserts to subzero arctic icefields.

DROPSHIPS

Because interstellar JumpShips must avoid entering the heart of a solar system, they must "dock" in space at a considerable distance from a system's inhabited worlds. DropShips were developed for interplanetary travel. As the name implies, a DropShip is attached to hardpoints on the JumpShip's drive core, later to be dropped from the parent vessel after in-system entry. Though incapable of FTL travel, DropShips are highly maneuverable, well-armed and sufficiently aerodynamic to take off from and land on a planetary surface. The journey from the jump point to the inhabited worlds of a system usually requires a normal-space journey of several days or weeks, depending on the type of star.

FLAMER

Flamethrowers are a small but time-honored anti-infantry weapon in vehicular arsenals. Whether fusion-based or fuel-based, flamers spew fire in a tight beam that "splashes" against a target, igniting almost anything it touches.

GAUSS RIFLE

This weapon uses magnetic coils to accelerate a solid nickel-ferrous slug about the size of a football at an enemy target, inflicting massive damage through sheer kinetic impact at long range and with little heat. However, the accelerator coils and the slug's supersonic speed mean that while the Gauss rifle is smokeless and lacks the flash of an autocannon, it has a much more potent report that can shatter glass.

INDUSTRIALMECH

Also known as WorkMechs or UtilityMechs, they are large, bipedal or quadrupedal machines used for industrial purposes (hence the name). They are similar in shape to BattleMechs, which they predate, and feature many of the same technologies, but are built for non-combat tasks such as construction, farming, and policing.

JUMPSHIPS

Interstellar travel is accomplished via JumpShips, first developed in the twenty-second century. These somewhat ungainly vessels consist of a long, thin drive core and a sail resembling an enormous parasol, which can extend up to a kilometer in width. The ship is named for its ability to "jump" instantaneously across vast distances of space. After making its jump, the ship cannot travel until it has recharged by gathering up more solar energy.

The JumpShip's enormous sail is constructed from a special metal that absorbs vast quantities of electromagnetic energy from the nearest star. When it has soaked up enough energy, the sail transfers it to the drive core, which converts it into a space-twisting field. An instant later, the ship arrives at the next jump point, a distance of up to thirty light-years. This field is known as hyperspace, and its discovery opened to mankind the gateway to the stars.

JumpShips never land on planets. Interplanetary travel is carried out by DropShips, vessels that are attached to the JumpShip until arrival at the jump point.

LASER

An acronym for "Light Amplification through Stimulated Emission of Radiation." When used as a weapon, the laser damages the target by concentrating extreme heat onto a small area. BattleMech lasers are designated as small, medium or large. Lasers are also available as shoulder-fired weapons operating from a portable backpack power unit. Certain range-finders and targeting equipment also employ low-level lasers.

LRM

Abbreviation for "Long-Range Missile," an indirect-fire missile with a high-explosive warhead.

MACHINE GUN

A small autocannon intended for anti-personnel assaults. Typically non-armor-penetrating, machine guns are often best used against infantry, as they can spray a large area with relatively inexpensive fire.

PARTICLE PROJECTION CANNON (PPC)

One of the most powerful and long-range energy weapons on the battlefield, a PPC fires a stream of charged particles that outwardly functions as a bright blue laser, but also throws off enough static discharge to resemble a bolt of manmade lightning. The kinetic and heat impact of a PPC is enough to cause the vaporization of armor and structure alike, and most PPCs have the power to kill a pilot in his machine through an armor-penetrating headshot.

SRM

The abbreviation for "Short-Range Missile," a direct-trajectory missile with high-explosive or armor-piercing explosive warheads. They have a range of less than one kilometer and are only reliably accurate at ranges of less than 300 meters. They are more powerful, however, than LRMs.

SUCCESSOR LORDS

After the fall of the first Star League, the remaining members of the High Council each asserted his or her right to become First Lord. Their star empires became known as the Successor States and the rulers as Successor Lords. The Clan Invasion temporarily interrupted centuries of warfare known as the Succession Wars, which first began in 2786.

BATTLETECH ERAS

The *BattleTech* universe is a living, vibrant entity that grows each year as more sourcebooks and fiction are published. A dynamic universe, its setting and characters evolve over time within a highly detailed continuity framework, bringing everything to life in a way a static game universe cannot match.

To help quickly and easily convey the timeline of the universe—and to allow a player to easily "plug in" a given novel or sourcebook—we've divided *BattleTech* into eight major eras.

STAR LEAGUE
(Present–2780)

Ian Cameron, ruler of the Terran Hegemony, concludes decades of tireless effort with the creation of the Star League, a political and military alliance between all Great Houses and the Hegemony. Star League armed forces immediately launch the Reunification War, forcing the Periphery realms to join. For the next two centuries, humanity experiences a golden age across the thousand light-years of human-occupied space known as the Inner Sphere. It also sees the creation of the most powerful military in human history.

(This era also covers the centuries before the founding of the Star League in 2571, most notably the Age of War.)

SUCCESSION WARS
(2781–3049)

Every last member of First Lord Richard Cameron's family is killed during a coup launched by Stefan Amaris. Following the thirteen-year war to unseat him, the rulers of each of the five Great Houses disband the Star League. General Aleksandr Kerensky departs with eighty percent of the Star League Defense Force beyond known space and the Inner Sphere collapses into centuries of warfare known as the Succession Wars that will eventually result in a massive loss of technology across most worlds.

CLAN INVASION
(3050–3061)

A mysterious invading force strikes the coreward region of the Inner Sphere. The invaders, called the Clans, are descendants of Kerensky's SLDF troops, forged into a society dedicated to becoming the greatest fighting force in history. With vastly superior technology and warriors, the Clans conquer world after world. Eventually this outside threat will forge a new Star League, something hundreds of years of warfare failed to accomplish. In addition, the Clans will act as a catalyst for a technological renaissance.

CIVIL WAR
(3062–3067)

The Clan threat is eventually lessened with the complete destruction of a Clan. With that massive external threat apparently neutralized, internal conflicts explode around the Inner Sphere. House Liao conquers its former Commonality, the St. Ives Compact; a rebellion of military units belonging to House Kurita sparks a war with their powerful border enemy, Clan Ghost Bear; the fabulously powerful Federated Commonwealth of House Steiner and House Davion collapses into five long years of bitter civil war.

JIHAD
(3067–3080)

Following the Federated Commonwealth Civil War, the leaders of the Great Houses meet and disband the new Star League, declaring it a sham. The pseudo-religious Word of Blake—a splinter group of ComStar, the protectors and controllers of interstellar communication—launch the Jihad: an interstellar war that pits every faction against each other and even against themselves, as weapons of mass destruction are used for the first time in centuries while new and frightening technologies are also unleashed.

DARK AGE
(3081–3150)

Under the guidance of Devlin Stone, the Republic of the Sphere is born at the heart of the Inner Sphere following the Jihad. One of the more extensive periods of peace begins to break out as the 32nd century dawns. The factions, to one degree or another, embrace disarmament, and the massive armies of the Succession Wars begin to fade. However, in 3132 eighty percent of interstellar communications collapses, throwing the universe into chaos. Wars erupt almost immediately, and the factions begin rebuilding their armies.

ILCLAN
(3151–present)

The once-invulnerable Republic of the Sphere lies in ruins, torn apart by the Great Houses and the Clans as they wage war against each other on a scale not seen in nearly a century. Mercenaries flourish once more, selling their might to the highest bidder. As Fortress Republic collapses, the Clans race toward Terra to claim their long-denied birthright and create a supreme authority that will fulfill the dream of Aleksandr Kerensky and rule the Inner Sphere by any means necessary: The ilClan.

CLAN HOMEWORLDS
(2786–present)

In 2784, General Aleksandr Kerensky launched Operation Exodus, and led most of the Star League Defense Force out of the Inner Sphere in a search for a new world, far away from the strife of the Great Houses. After more than two years and thousands of light years, they arrived at the Pentagon Worlds. Over the next two-and-a-half centuries, internal dissent and civil war led to the creation of a brutal new society—the Clans. And in 3049, they returned to the Inner Sphere with one goal—the complete conquest of the Great Houses.

LOOKING FOR MORE HARD HITTING BATTLETECH FICTION?

WE'LL GET YOU RIGHT BACK INTO THE BATTLE!

Catalyst Game Labs brings you the very best in *BattleTech* fiction, available at most ebook retailers, including Amazon, Apple Books, Kobo, Barnes & Noble, and more!

NOVELS

1. *Decision at Thunder Rift* by William H. Keith Jr.
2. *Mercenary's Star* by William H. Keith Jr.
3. *The Price of Glory* by William H. Keith, Jr.
4. *Warrior: En Garde* by Michael A. Stackpole
5. *Warrior: Riposte* by Michael A. Stackpole
6. *Warrior: Coupé* by Michael A. Stackpole
7. Wolves on the Border by Robert N. Charrette
8. *Heir to the Dragon* by Robert N. Charrette
9. *Lethal Heritage* (The Blood of Kerensky, Volume 1) by Michael A. Stackpole
10. *Blood Legacy* (The Blood of Kerensky, Volume 2) by Michael A. Stackpole
11. *Lost Destiny* (The Blood of Kerensky, Volume 3) by Michael A. Stackpole
12. *Way of the Clans* (Legend of the Jade Phoenix, Volume 1) by Robert Thurston
13. *Bloodname* (Legend of the Jade Phoenix, Volume 2) by Robert Thurston
14. *Falcon Guard* (Legend of the Jade Phoenix, Volume 3) by Robert Thurston
15. *Wolf Pack* by Robert N. Charrette
16. *Main Event* by James D. Long
17. *Natural Selection* by Michael A. Stackpole
18. *Assumption of Risk* by Michael A. Stackpole
19. *Blood of Heroes* by Andrew Keith
20. *Close Quarters* by Victor Milán
21. *Far Country* by Peter L. Rice
22. *D.R.T.* by James D. Long
23. *Tactics of Duty* by William H. Keith
24. *Bred for War* by Michael A. Stackpole
25. *I Am Jade Falcon* by Robert Thurston
26. *Highlander Gambit* by Blaine Lee Pardoe
27. *Hearts of Chaos* by Victor Milán
28. *Operation Excalibur* by William H. Keith
29. *Malicious Intent* by Michael A. Stackpole
30. *Black Dragon* by Victor Milán
31. *Impetus of War* by Blaine Lee Pardoe
32. *Double-Blind* by Loren L. Coleman
33. *Binding Force* by Loren L. Coleman
34. *Exodus Road* (Twilight of the Clans, Volume 1) by Blaine Lee Pardoe
35. *Grave Covenant* ((Twilight of the Clans, Volume 2) by Michael A. Stackpole

76. *Daughter of the Dragon* by Ilsa J. Bick
77. *Heretic's Faith* by Randall N. Bills
78. *Fortress Republic* by Loren L. Coleman
79. *Blood Avatar* by Ilsa J. Bick
80. *Trial by Chaos* by J. Steven York
81. *Principles of Desolation* by Jason M. Hardy and Randall N. Bills
82. *Wolf Hunters* by Kevin Killiany
83. *Surrender Your Dreams* by Blaine Lee Pardoe
84. *Dragon Rising* by Ilsa J. Bick
85. *Masters of War* by Michael A. Stackpole
86. *A Rending of Falcons* by Victor Milán
87. *Pandora's Gambit* by Randall N. Bills
88. *Fire at Will* by Blaine Lee Pardoe
89. *The Last Charge* by Jason M. Hardy
90. *To Ride the Chimera* by Kevin Killiany
91. *A Bonfire of Worlds* by Steven Mohan, Jr.
92. *Isle of the Blessed* by Steven Mohan, Jr.
93. *Embers of War* by Jason Schmetzer
94. *Betrayal of Ideals* by Blaine Lee Pardoe
95. *Forever Faithful* by Blaine Lee Pardoe
96. *Kell Hounds Ascendant* by Michael A. Stackpole
97. *Redemption Rift* by Jason Schmetzer
98. *Grey Watch Protocol (The Highlander Covenant, Book One)* by Michael J. Ciaravella
99. *Honor's Gauntlet* by Bryan Young
100. *Icons of War* by Craig A. Reed, Jr.
101. *Children of Kerensky* by Blaine Lee Pardoe
102. *Hour of the Wolf* by Blaine Lee Pardoe
103. *Fall From Glory (Founding of the Clans, Book One)* by Randall N. Bills
104. *Paid in Blood (The Highlander Covenant, Book Two)* by Michael J. Ciaravella
105. *Blood Will Tell* by Jason Schmetzer
106. *Hunting Season* by Philip A. Lee
107. *A Rock and a Hard Place* by William H. Keith, Jr.
108. *Visions of Rebirth* (Founding of the Clans, Book Two) by Randall N. Bills
109. *No Substitute for Victory* by Blaine Lee Pardoe
110. *Redemption Rites* by Jason Schmetzer
111. *Land of Dreams* (Founding of the Clans, Book Three) by Randall N. Bills
112. *A Question of Survival* by Bryan Young
113. *Jaguar's Leap* by Reed Bishop

YOUNG ADULT NOVELS

1. *The Nellus Academy Incident* by Jennifer Brozek
2. *Iron Dawn (Rogue Academy, Book 1)* by Jennifer Brozek
3. *Ghost Hour (Rogue Academy, Book 2)* by Jennifer Brozek
4. *Crimson Night (Rogue Academy, Book 3)* by Jennifer Brozek

OMNIBUSES

1. *The Gray Death Legion Trilogy* by William H. Keith, Jr.
2. *The Blood of Kerensky Trilogy* by Michael A. Stackpole

NOVELLAS/SHORT STORIES

1. *Lion's Roar* by Steven Mohan, Jr.
2. *Sniper* by Jason Schmetzer
3. *Eclipse* by Jason Schmetzer
4. *Hector* by Jason Schmetzer
5. *The Frost Advances (Operation Ice Storm, Part 1)* by Jason Schmetzer
6. *The Winds of Spring (Operation Ice Storm, Part 2)* by Jason Schmetzer
7. *Instrument of Destruction (Ghost Bear's Lament, Part 1)*
      by Steven Mohan, Jr.
8. *The Fading Call of Glory (Ghost Bear's Lament, Part 2)* by Steven Mohan, Jr.
9. *Vengeance* by Jason Schmetzer
10. *A Splinter of Hope* by Philip A. Lee
11. *The Anvil* by Blaine Lee Pardoe
12. *A Splinter of Hope/The Anvil* (omnibus)
13. *Not the Way the Smart Money Bets (Kell Hounds Ascendant #1)*
      by Michael A. Stackpole
14. *A Tiny Spot of Rebellion (Kell Hounds Ascendant #2)*
      by Michael A. Stackpole
15. *A Clever Bit of Fiction (Kell Hounds Ascendant #3)* by Michael A. Stackpole
16. *Break-Away (Proliferation Cycle #1)* by Ilsa J. Bick
17. *Prometheus Unbound (Proliferation Cycle #2)* by Herbert A. Beas II
18. *Nothing Ventured (Proliferation Cycle #3)* by Christoffer Trossen
19. *Fall Down Seven Times, Get Up Eight (Proliferation Cycle #4)* by Randall N. Bills
20. *A Dish Served Cold (Proliferation Cycle #5)*
      by Chris Hartford and Jason M. Hardy
21. *The Spider Dances (Proliferation Cycle #6)* by Jason Schmetzer
22. *Shell Games* by Jason Schmetzer
23. *Divided We Fall* by Blaine Lee Pardoe
24. *The Hunt for Jardine (Forgotten Worlds, Part One)* by Herbert A. Beas II
25. *Rock of the Republic* by Blaine Lee Pardoe
26. *Finding Jardine (Forgotten Worlds, Part Two)* by Herbert A. Beas II
27. *The Trickster (Proliferation Cycle #7)* by Blaine Lee Pardoe
28. *The Price of Duty* by Jason Schmetzer
29. *Elements of Treason: Duty* by Craig A. Reed, Jr.
30. *Mercenary's Honor* by Jason Schmetzer
31. *Elements of Treason: Opportunity* by Craig A. Reed, Jr.

ANTHOLOGIES

1. *The Corps (BattleCorps Anthology, Volume 1)* edited by Loren. L. Coleman
2. *First Strike (BattleCorps Anthology, Volume 2)* edited by Loren L. Coleman
3. *Weapons Free (BattleCorps Anthology, Volume 3)* edited by Jason Schmetzer
4. *Onslaught: Tales from the Clan Invasion* edited by Jason Schmetzer
5. *Edge of the Storm* by Jason Schmetzer
6. *Fire for Effect (BattleCorps Anthology, Volume 4)* edited by Jason Schmetzer
7. *Chaos Born (Chaos Irregulars, Book 1)* by Kevin Killiany
8. *Chaos Formed (Chaos Irregulars, Book 2)* by Kevin Killiany
9. *Counterattack (BattleCorps Anthology, Volume 5)* edited by Jason Schmetzer
10. *Front Lines (BattleCorps Anthology Volume 6)*
    edited by Jason Schmetzer and Philip A. Lee
11. *Legacy* edited by John Helfers and Philip A. Lee
12. *Kill Zone (BattleCorps Anthology Volume 7)* edited by Philip A. Lee
13. *Gray Markets (A BattleCorps Anthology),*
    edited by Jason Schmetzer and Philip A. Lee
14. *Slack Tide (A BattleCorps Anthology),*
    edited by Jason Schmetzer and Philip A. Lee
15. *The Battle of Tukayyid* edited by John Helfers
16. *The Mercenary Life* by Randall N. Bills
17. *The Proliferation Cycle* edited by John Helfers and Philip A. Lee
18. *No Greater Honor (The Complete Eridani Light Horse Chronicles)*
    edited by John Helfers and Philip A. Lee
19. *Marauder* by Lance Scarinci

MAGAZINES

1. *Shrapnel Issues #01–#10*

Made in the USA
Columbia, SC
05 November 2022

70515542R00100